Everette: Driverton 1

The Barrington Billionaires
Book 13

Ruth Cardello

Author Contact
website: RuthCardello.com
email: rcardello@ruthcardello.com
Facebook: Author Ruth Cardello
Twitter: RuthieCardello

Copyright

Driverton's sweetest man is on a mission to become a hero.

After graduating from "Bradford's School for Sobriety and Success," AKA months of military style, intense physical and mental training, Everette Morin is saving lives. Joining forces with both Bradford Wilson and Cooper Landon, Everette is locating, retrieving, and returning missing children.

Shelby Adams is reeling from the loss of her parents and a breakup with someone who'd promised to always be there for: she's hit rock bottom.

She's not looking for a man—not even a big, strong one with an amazing smile and the ability to make her laugh.

It'll take the whole Driverton crew to lift her up, turn her life around, and show her that sometimes even heroes need saving.

Dedication

This book is dedicated to all the humble heroes,
the ones who, without fanfare, show love and kindness daily
to all those around them.
You make the world a better place.

Note to my readers

Welcome back to Driverton. It's a fictitious town in Maine, so small it's often forgotten on maps. *Loathing a Landon* was the first book set in this town. I enjoyed visiting it so much that Driverton is the setting of the next three books in the Barrington Billionaire series.

Driverton is best described by Mrs. Williams: "I'm ashamed to say I used to think horrible things about small towns. I've learned, though, that they're only as good or as bad as the people in them. Driverton has a tough reputation in the local area. We don't put up with nonsense from outsiders. But there's a difference between being nice and being kind. The people in this town won't talk pretty to you. If your car breaks down going through here, they'll tell you all the things you should have done that could have prevented that from happening, but then they'll take you in, feed you a good meal, and get you back on your way if you have the manners to thank them for it. But you bring a bad attitude here—we'll tow your broken-ass car to the town line and leave it there."

Everette, Levi, and Ollie are the rowdy but sexy and good-hearted single men of Driverton. I hope you enjoy the wild ride of each of them finally meeting their match.

Chapter One

Shelby

"DO YOU WANT me to come to you?" Megan, my best friend, asked again, clearly unhappy with the vague answer I'd given the first time. "I have travel points; I could probably catch a short flight tonight."

I shook my head, wishing I'd said the video option on my phone wasn't working. The past twenty-four hours had been rough, and it was impossible to lie about that when Megan could see how ragged I looked. "I'm okay. At least, I will be. I just need a little time."

"Have you spoken to him since—"

"No." Emotion thickened my voice. "There was nothing left to say. He was right to ask me to leave. I didn't really want to be with him. I just didn't want to be alone. I never actually settled in. All I had to do was pack up my luggage and go. You told me it was too soon, that I shouldn't have said yes, that it was a mistake . . ."

"Shelby, I hate that I was right. Where did you stay last night?"

"In my car. It wasn't that bad, actually."

"That's not safe. Come home—"

"No. I don't want to go back." When the words came out more vehemently than I'd meant them to, I added, "I'm sorry."

"Don't be. I understand why you don't want to be here anymore, and of course you didn't want to be alone after what happened. Unfortunately, some men take advantage of women when they're struggling. Jeff swept in, saying all the right things. Hell, in your situation, I would have gone with him too. I'm not judging you."

"I know." Megan was a better friend than I deserved. She'd been that way since we met in grade school during a ballet class neither of us enjoyed. We'd both considered being forced to wear pink tights and remain quiet hell on earth. After a few weeks, we'd quit and joined a soccer team together—and ruled the field side by side for years.

"Help me help you. What can I do?" Megan asked gently.

"Do you have a time machine?" It was a sad attempt at joking about something that would never be funny.

"I wish I did." After a pause, she asked, "Where are you staying? Do you have a plan?"

"There's no shortage of hotels in Rhode Island. I'll find something."

"Text me as soon as you choose one."

"I will."

"You're going to be okay, Shelby."

"That's what I'm telling myself."

"I'm only a phone call away. It doesn't matter what time

it is. I'll pick up. You're not alone."

I wiped tears from the corners of my eyes. "Thank you. I love you, Megan."

"My offer to come to you stands. Today. Tomorrow. Next week. If you need me, I'll come."

Nodding while trying not to burst into tears, I said, "Time on my own will be good for me. I need to figure out who I am now and what I want to do."

"Every day will be a little easier. I promise."

That didn't seem possible, but I nodded because she needed to believe that. "I'm going to go now." I turned my phone so she could see the view before me. "Look at that lake. Isn't it beautiful? I might end up emptying my savings account to stay here, but it's the kind of peacefulness I need. Hopefully I can find a place on the water."

"I'm doing a search now. I'll text what I find."

God, I loved her. "What would I do without you?"

"You'll never have to find out. I'm not going anywhere. And neither are you. You've been my strength so many times in the past. I hope I'm half as good at supporting you as you've always been for me."

I fought back a sob. "I'm saying goodbye before you make me ugly bawl in public."

"Call or text me tonight. Promise?"

"Promise." With that, I ended the call and replaced the phone in my back pocket. I found a bench and sat for a long time, trying to empty my mind as I looked out over the water.

Unwelcome voices intruded. One was from a young female asking how long they would have to stay in that town before they headed down to New York City. The male voice that answered promised her it wouldn't be very long and that the wait would be worth it. He said he was still setting up agents for her to meet when they got there. It was better, he said, to wait one more day and go down when all her appointments were scheduled.

I didn't hear her response because they'd walked out of earshot, but I was tempted to run after them and warn her that men promised all kinds of things they had no intention of following through on. I didn't, though, because my view of both men and the way the world worked was severely tainted by my current circumstances.

Five months, six days, and ten hours ago the life I'd known had ended with one phone call. I'd been working an overtime shift at my airport job, feeling lucky to have one with flex hours as well as the ability to nearly double my pay by picking up holiday hours. My parents had been proud when I'd graduated from college and even prouder when I'd become a logistics manager for a major airline. Their relief had been tangible when I'd told them even though I wanted to get my own apartment, the job would keep me local to them.

My life plan had been falling perfectly into place, until that one call. Every single detail of that day was forever burned into my memory. Just when I would think I'd successfully put it out of my thoughts, it would wash over me, tumbling me under like a rogue wave sweeping someone off an otherwise peaceful beach.

I would find myself right back there in the office, smelling the stale scent of the rug, feeling the weight of the beige walls closing in on me while I clutched my phone with shaking hands.

"Ms. Adams, there's been an accident . . ."

But it hadn't been an accident. Not really. As my parents slept, someone had broken into their home with the intention of robbing them. There'd been a struggle; my mother had been injured, my father shot, and a fire started. The police report included a death certificate for not just my parents but also their assailant. It was thought that the man who'd broken into my parents' home hadn't wanted to leave empty-handed and had, despite the fire, attempted to gather their valuables. They found his body in my father's home office with his pockets full of credit cards and pieces of jewelry that weren't worth much at all.

The next few weeks were a blur. There'd been meetings with the police, a lawyer, and a funeral director. Friends and family tried to be supportive, but all I wanted was to be alone.

One day, the family of the man who died trying to rob my parents showed up on my social media feed. They'd made a video claiming their son was the real victim because my parents had decided to fight instead of fleeing. They implied they had proof that my father had started the fire deliberately to kill their son. The story went viral on social media.

There was no proof and their accusation was baseless. According to the coroner, although my father had been shot, he and my mother were still alive when the fire started. Accelerant had been poured in the hallway where my parents were found. The investigating officer said the intruder had likely wanted to cover the crime with a fire, but hadn't understood how fast the home would fill with smoke and how quickly it could turn deadly.

When the lawn in front of my parents' home started filling with flowers from people mourning the young man rather than my parents—it was too much for me. Megan stepped in and helped me sort out my parents' insurance policy and hire contractors to fix the house. I found a Realtor for when the house was ready to sell and walked away, no longer wanting anything to do with the place I'd once thought would always represent home to me.

Megan was a practical soul. She said people mourn for the story they know and that it wasn't a battle I could win. Public opinion had been swayed and, in the end, didn't change anything. She was right. I couldn't hate the family of the man who'd robbed my parents. They'd lost a son, a brother, a cousin . . .

But I couldn't stomach the physical shows of sympathy for that family while there was none for mine. Therapy helped a little with that, but I soon stopped being angry and just went numb.

Then came Jeff.

I'd met him a few years earlier when his flight had been delayed and I'd bumped into him at the airport. We'd had dinner together and sex the next time he'd come to town. No, it hadn't been a hot and heavy affair. Looking back, I'd say we were friends who sometimes had sex. But when he'd heard what had happened and opened his home to me—it had felt like a lifeline thrown to someone drowning. He'd promised things would get better and that he'd always be there for me.

I quit the job I loved and went to live with him in Rhode Island. I brought almost nothing with me because there was very little about my old life I wanted to keep. Everything that mattered was gone.

Yesterday, four months after I moved in with him, Jeff had sat me down and we'd had the conversation no one wants. It wasn't working. He apologized profusely, making it impossible to hate him. He said he'd thought he could help me, but I wasn't doing anything to move forward. I hadn't gotten a job, made any friends, or even been intimate with him. He couldn't do it anymore, and I didn't blame him because I didn't want to be with me anymore either.

I'd tried.

I'd gone through the motions of finding a job. I'd posted my résumé, gone to interviews, but every time a potential employer showed interest, I found a reason I couldn't take the job. It was the same when it came to connecting with his friends. Pretending to be happy was exhausting; it was easier to be on my own. And him? I *wanted* to want him. We'd slept in the same bed, talked about wanting to be together, but in the end he was too good of a man to push himself on me and I wasn't interested in sex anymore.

I should have corrected Megan when she'd lumped him with men who took advantage of women when they were struggling. If anyone was guilty of taking advantage of anyone, it was me. I'd moved into his house like an entitled stray cat, expecting three meals a day simply for existing and not messing on the carpet.

As I sat there looking out across the water, I knew Jeff had done me a favor. I did need to pick myself up and start living again.

And I would.

As soon as I figured out how.

Chapter Two

Everette

UP EARLY AND on my first solo assignment, I started the day with a five-mile run, a feat that wouldn't have been possible for me months earlier. A lot of things had changed since my friend Cooper Davis had become Cooper Davis *Landon*. It was not every day someone in my hometown went from being broke like the rest of us, to announcing his family was filthy rich. We'd always known Cooper had secrets. He'd been young and on the run from something horrific when he'd shown up in Driverton. We'd taken him in and made him one of our own.

Being wealthy had sounded more tempting before I'd heard the story of how Cooper's uncle had torn the Landon family to shreds out of greed. Money certainly hadn't brought much good to the Landons. Since being reunited, they were still patching their relationships back together.

My family might have always struggled to pay the bills, but we were tight. The same could be said about all those who lived in Driverton. It was a town in Maine so small it was often left off maps. Long, cold winters forced us to rely on each other for survival and that fostered the kind of trust outsiders couldn't understand.

Bradford Wilson had come to Driverton to find Cooper Landon, but had stayed because he and his wife, Joanna, fell in love with our community. In the words of Mrs. Williams, everyone in town's second mother, "There is always room at our table, but we don't suffer fools gladly so leave your ego at the door." I can attest to how much she meant those words. She didn't sugarcoat her opinions and she had standards of behavior she'd hold even God to if he came for a visit.

No one had been surprised when she'd told Bradford to use his military training to sober up the young men in town—me included. Bradford's big job with the CIA? Well, she said, that should mean he's smart enough to figure out how to get her adult son, Ollie, to balance working at his restaurant with helping around the house more. Fences needed mending. The electrical needed updating. No, she didn't want money to have it fixed. Why did anyone in town need money when they had able-bodied young ones who simply needed to put down their beers and step up?

She was right. Levi, Ollie, and I had all given up on being more than we were, and drinking ourselves into a stupor had become where we found our joy. Small towns, for all their strengths, can do that to a person. I loved my family, loved my friends, had never resented working to support my parents and siblings, but my life had felt as small as Driverton was. And, I'll admit, there were times I'd felt trapped by all the same things I loved about it. My dreams? I hadn't allowed myself any. I was where I needed to be, doing what needed to be done. Drinking had been my way of freeing myself from the weight of that.

Bradford was the first person I'd ever confessed that to—sober, at least. He'd offered to train me and my friends, just like Mrs. Williams had instructed him to. I was the only one so far to agree to it. To understand why none of us immediately jumped at the opportunity, you'd have to know Bradford. I've always been referred to as a gentle giant. Bradford was close to my height and breadth, but his face and body were scarred and his eyes went cold sometimes. You could sense that he was someone who could take another's life, bury him in a back field, and never fucking say a word about it.

Cooper said Bradford was the person the government sent in to save someone when the situation was too sensitive or volatile for them to use a Special Forces unit. That sounded far-fetched until you got to know Bradford.

Yep. I could imagine him doing whatever was necessary to save someone. He was the kind of hero people don't like to admit the world needs. Before I agreed to work with him, I gave him a few tastes of the lifestyle Levi, Ollie, and I were reluctant to give up.

Tipsy by noon on weekdays? If your chores are done, absolutely.

Pass out drunk on the weekends? Race you to it.

Inebriated Bradford was fucking hilarious, but he could also tell a story that would have a grown man ready to bawl into his beer over the heinous side of humanity and then be just as ready to go to war to protect the innocent. When I'd learned that Cooper had been working with Sheriff Tom to locate and retrieve runaways, I'd expressed a desire to help them. It was only after getting to know Bradford that I understood how much I'd need to learn.

Cooper and Bradford had bonded quickly because they had a lot in common. Both had perfected extraction without detection. They practiced the art of remaining invisible while tracking their target. They used burner phones, clothing designed to confuse AI from recognizing them, paid everything in cash, created aliases, drove cars that couldn't be traced, and were careful to leave no fingerprints.

The only difference? Cooper and Sheriff Tom held to a code of letting the justice system deal with everything beyond saving the runaway. Bradford had seen more, and his moral code wasn't as clear. Over too many shots of moonshine, Bradford admitted that meeting Joanna was all that had saved him from becoming no different than the monsters he'd unalived.

Could I train with a man like that?

Should I?

It was a question I'd asked myself many times before I decided his desire to move to Driverton was revealing. He needed a community as much as the world needed him. And, just like Cooper, we made him one of us.

He offered to pay me while I trained with him, but I'd been raised too proud for that. I supported my family by selling chainsaw-carved wooden structures. It was manual labor I'd always done with ease. I told myself I could do that around my training schedule. I was wrong. Training with

Bradford was like boot camp. He had me up at dawn running until I threw up. I lifted weights until I couldn't, honed my ability to shoot, and learned to stealthily scale almost anything. There was no time to consider meeting Levi or Ollie for a drink and I fell into bed exhausted each day.

At the end of my first week, Bradford showed up at my house unexpectedly and caught me trying and failing to cut a bear sculpture. My arms were shaking so much I kept fucking up the lines. He took the chainsaw from me and asked me to guide him through how to do it. That was when I knew Bradford really was one of us. In Driverton, people stepped up when someone was in need. We didn't do it for the glory or with any expectation of compensation. We did it because that's what a community does for its own.

Now, that sculpture wasn't worth shit, but I'd never tell Bradford or anyone else that. I hid it in our back barn and didn't speak of it again. My workouts with Bradford became slightly less intense after that, enough so I could finish the projects I'd lined up while becoming more fit than my ass had ever imagined I could.

When I was ready, Cooper let me shadow him as he tracked a twelve-year-old girl who'd gotten in a physical altercation with her mother's boyfriend and had run away. We found her several states away, miraculously safe, hitch-hiking her way to her father. She wasn't happy to be *rescued*, but Cooper talked her into trusting us. We took her to her father, helped him secure legal representation, and when we left her, I'd felt on top of the world. Cooper had set up counseling for the family and the boyfriend was being handled by the courts. Justice prevailed.

When Bradford offered to let me join him as he searched for an infant that had been snatched from a playground, I expected to return from that job with the same optimism. What I experienced was a life-changing, horrifying nightmare where crimes like that were perpetrated not by one sick person, but by networks of them—*for profit*. There was no happy ending. There was tracking, location, retrieval, carnage, then cover-up.

I didn't kill anyone, but I did shoot when shot at and covered Bradford's back while he cut through anyone who stood between him and the child. Part of me was repulsed by his methods, but when he came out of the house and handed me the child—I decided there had to be room in heaven for him. There had to be. If not, I'd endure the fire to ensure no one like him ever suffered alone.

As I ran, I brought my focus back to the reason I was in Rhode Island. A call had come in to Sheriff Tom regarding a fifteen-year-old girl from Connecticut who'd been categorized as a runaway. Alexia Paine's parents insisted she'd always been impulsive, but wasn't abused and hadn't given any indication that she might not be happy. I'd been offered this as my first solo assignment.

Evan Lamb was my alias. I was a small-time real estate investor looking for vacation rental properties to buy. My imaginary fiancée and I were also looking for a nice town to relocate to, so my cover for asking questions was that I wanted to get a feel for different towns before bringing them up to my fiancée for her final approval.

Time spent in Alexia's hometown had given me the opportunity to speak to some of her friends. They confessed that Alexia had been seeing someone she hadn't told her parents about. He was someone from out of town with a nice car. They hadn't told the police about him because they didn't want her to get in trouble with her parents, then as time went on they'd been afraid to get themselves in trouble because they'd held back that information.

All they had was a first name, Curtis, and he drove a silver sedan with stickers from different states on the back window. One of Alexia's friends had been present when Alexia had been on the phone with him and thought she remembered him talking about a lake house his family owned in Rhode Island. The number of the person Alexia had spoken to came back as a burner phone. This was no amateur. Bradford warned against going to the police. Whoever had taken Alexia thought they'd gotten away with it. If they saw her face on the television they might eliminate her and move on to an easier target. Or, just as bad, they could cover their tracks so well we might never find them. Bradford offered to join the search, and I didn't refuse. Whoever Alexia was with, he was likely dangerous and, if we didn't stop him, Alexia wouldn't be his last snatch.

The final tower Alexia's phone had connected to was in northern Rhode Island a few days ago. Bradford was following a lead to a lake south of the one I was canvassing. During my run, I stopped to speak to everyone I came across. If they didn't fit the profile of someone who might be involved, I showed them a photo of Alexia and asked them if they'd seen her. There was a risk involved in that, but we didn't have the luxury of time. Sometimes, according to Bradford, a man had to put aside his training and trust his instincts.

I slowed my speed as I saw a lone figure sitting on a bench, looking out over the water. Long brown hair similar to the teen I was searching for, but as I approached, the person looked up and my hope that it might be her disappeared.

The woman on the bench was beautiful, but most likely in her mid-twenties . . . and crying. *Shit.*

Wiping the sweat from my forehead on the short sleeve of my T-shirt, I debated whether I should leave her to whatever she was dealing with or intervene. She'd obviously sought this secluded location out of a desire to be alone. Still, if I'd learned anything over the past few months, it was that clues could come in many forms and from the least expected sources. What made Cooper and Bradford successful in searches where others failed was their tenacious natures. They didn't give up. Neither of them would walk by this woman without determining if she'd seen Alexia.

When I came to a stop close to the bench, the woman stood and wiped at her cheeks. The expression on her face was one a smart man recognized. She didn't know me and there was no one around. Her hand went in her bag and my guess was it would resurface with a can of Mace if I took another step toward her.

I shot her my most charming smile. "I've been running for so long I think I've gotten myself turned around. Is the boat ramp beyond the trees?"

"I have no idea," she answered. "Sorry." She turned to leave, but kept her hand in her bag and glanced at me more than once to make sure I wasn't following her.

I stayed where I was, but said, "Hey. Can I ask you a question?"

From a distance of ten feet or so, she turned to face me. "I don't know this area."

"I promise I won't quiz you about landmarks. I just want to show you something." When my hand went to my back pocket to pull out the photo, her eyes widened, she shook her head then turned and bolted to her car.

Real smooth. I have to learn to do this better.

I couldn't judge her for fleeing. Had I wanted to, I could easily have overpowered her, Mace or no Mace. She was smart to not want to be in a secluded area with a stranger. Still, it made me sad that she knew that. Had someone hurt her? Was that why she was crying? She hadn't appeared bruised or injured, but there'd been a sadness in her eyes that had gutted me.

I knew nothing about her.

She wasn't why I was there.

Still, I couldn't leave before I knew she'd made it safely to her car and that it started without a problem.

Chapter Three

Shelby

I LOOKED MYSELF in the eye in the mirror of the bathroom of the one-bedroom suite Megan found for me in a waterfront bed-and-breakfast. *Stop. I'm fine. Nothing happened. I'm not afraid.*

I'm a strong, independent woman and can take care of myself, I repeated in my head again and again until my heart stopped racing and my hands unclenched at my sides. *I am not afraid of anyone.*

Closing my eyes briefly, I endured a wave of embarrassment as I remembered how I'd turned and literally ran to my car. *No wonder Jeff asked me to leave. I'm not right.*

What if this is the new me?

Will I always be this afraid?

Can I live like this?

I opened my eyes and gave myself a stern look. *I have to. Adams are not quitters. My father fought to protect my mother. He would have fought to protect me. If he was here he'd say something inspirational and tell me how much he loves me.*

Mom would have done the same.

Both of them would have told me I'm better than this.
I'll find a way to be.

Hugging myself, I walked out of the bathroom and looked around the pink and white room. The décor was similar to what I would have chosen when I was very young and somehow that was comforting. Megan had found a small bed-and-breakfast run by an older couple whose names I'd already forgotten. There one other guest, but when they'd told me about him, I'd already given in to a mini panic attack at my inability to remember their names and didn't listen to what they said about him.

Megan told me stress and trauma could affect a person's ability to concentrate. I would have allowed myself that excuse in the weeks that followed my parents' deaths, but months later? It was frustrating and disappointing. I wanted to be someone who remembered the names of adorable older couples and didn't turn and run as soon as a stranger approached me.

Who was this stranger I'd become?

The temptation to call Jeff and beg him to take me back was strong, but I didn't want to be that person either so I didn't allow myself to call. Instead I texted Megan photos of the bedroom and told her how amazing the place was. And, probably because she knew me better than anyone else in the world did, she sent back an overview of the place, including the names of both owners as well as the other guest and I burst into tears.

She loved me even when I couldn't find a reason to love myself. Sandy and Drew Allen. Evan Lamb. *Lamb? That doesn't sound scary.*

Outside of the movie The Silence of the Lambs.

But I won't think about that.

Lambs are timid and quiet.

Evan Lamb is probably sixty years old, soft and round. He's likely sitting in a room just like this, missing his wife and kids.

I'm safe.

There was a hand-printed card on a table near the door. It said lunch would be served in the dining room from eleven to one o'clock. A glance at the clock on the wall revealed lunch had already started. I hadn't eaten anything since I'd left Jeff's early the day before and my stomach rumbled.

I squared my shoulders and stuffed my phone in my back pocket while practicing what I'd say. *Sandy and Drew, thank you for this lovely meal. Evan, I hope your room is as nice as mine.*

No, I shouldn't say that last part.

It's better if I say nothing.

My stomach rumbled again so I made my way from my room down the stairs to the dining room I'd seen earlier when I'd checked in. "Hello, Mrs. Allen," I said when she met me in the hallway. She was still in the modest, flowered dress from earlier, but she'd draped a large white apron over the front of it.

She shot me a warm smile. "Sandy. Please. We're not so formal."

"Sandy. Of course. Am I on time for lunch?"

Her smile widened. "You are definitely on time. Tell me, are you single?"

I stiffened. "Sorry?"

She smoothed a gray curl back into the loose bun at the nape of her neck. "I hope you are, because I'm happily married but I'd be lying if I didn't say Evan Lamb is the best-looking man I've ever laid my eyes on. He says he's engaged, but engaged ain't married. So unless you have someone waiting for you back home, I'd go put on some makeup and something a little more revealing and thank me tomorrow."

"Wow." It was a lot to take in. "I don't have someone back home." *I don't even have a home.* "But, to me, engaged is as good as married. So, thank you for looking out for me, but I'm sure I'm not interested."

She shook her head. "You'll change your mind as soon as you see him. Hell, Drew is going to have the time of his life tonight just because I spent the day next to all that testosterone."

My cheeks flushed, but I laughed. My mother used to tease a blush out of me now and then by saying something about my father. "Sounds like Mr. Allen is a very lucky man."

"He sure is," Sandy said with a wink, then turned and led me into the dining room. "We only have one table. Sit where you'd like. I know where I'd sit if I were you."

The chuckle that had come out of me at her last comment died in my throat as soon as I met the gaze of the mountain of a man who rose to his feet as soon as I entered the room. Evan Lamb was the same man I'd run from a few hours earlier.

The low ceiling of the bed-and-breakfast made him seem even taller than he had by the lake. He'd showered and changed into jean shorts and a navy T-shirt that did little to hide how muscular he was. Earlier, I'd been embarrassed because he'd come across me while I'd been crying, then fear had taken hold. I hadn't taken the time to appreciate his square jaw, dark eyes, and easy smile. I wasn't about to admit it to Mrs. Allen, but he was the best-looking man I'd ever laid my eyes on too. There wasn't an inch of him that wasn't toned to perfection. And the testosterone Mrs. Allen had referenced? It was there in such abundance I was pretty certain a woman could get pregnant simply by standing too close to him.

Mrs. Allen waved a hand toward him then me. "Evan Lamb, this is Shelby Adams. Shelby, would you like coffee? Tea? Juice?"

Frozen where I was, I answered without looking away from Evan. "Tea, please."

"Great," she said. "Have a seat. I'll be right back with some. Evan, was one sandwich enough or would you like another?"

Holding my gaze, he answered, "I'd love another if it's no trouble."

She cackled. "I knew a man like you would have a healthy appetite."

Left alone, there was no way to avoid the awkwardness of coming face-to-face with someone I'd run from. I took a deep, fortifying breath as I tried to come up with something to extricate myself from the situation.

His expression softened. "I apologize for earlier. I didn't mean to intrude the way I did."

"You didn't." It was an automatic response that was so clearly a lie that I winced after voicing it. "I hope I didn't offend you by leaving the way I did. It was just that I'd gone there to be alone and . . ."

"And then I ran up on you."

"There was running on both sides."

He smiled at my joke and I relaxed a little. "I have a problem I hope you can help me with."

My guard went up again as I braced myself for his request. "Yes?"

"My mother raised me to never sit while a woman is standing."

That had me tilting my head to one side and asking myself if he was serious. He was. I chose a seat diagonal from him rather than directly across. He sat down right after I did. Unsure of what to say, I adjusted the silverware before me, rather than looking at him.

In a deep voice that sent confusing ripples of warmth through me, he said, "I'd be helping Mrs. Allen in the kitchen if she'd let me, but she threatened to smack me with a spoon if I tried."

I laughed and raised my gaze to meet his. "I'm sure she was joking."

"Not so sure she was."

Mrs. Allen was back with a tray. Evan stood to help her. She chastised him and told him to sit before he got in the way and made her spill something. Evan and I shared an amused look. Okay, so I could imagine her wielding a spoon if he entered her kitchen. Did Evan have any idea that some of Mrs. Allen's posturing was due to the fact that he was drop-dead gorgeous? I couldn't tell. He was certainly confident, but he didn't appear to have an ego that many would if they looked like him.

After serving each of us a drink and placing an assortment of sandwiches on a platter before us, Mrs. Allen told us to ring the bell on the table if we needed her then disappeared into the kitchen. The silence that followed was strained.

I spoke first. "So, Mrs. Allen told me you're engaged." I didn't blurt that out because I needed to remind myself that he was taken.

Okay, that was exactly why I'd done it.

He blinked a few times before answering, "I am."

"That's exciting." I forced enthusiasm into my voice.

"Yes."

He didn't light up at the mention of his fiancée and I didn't like that. Some men didn't take commitment seriously and I'd never understood why they married at all. My parents had been devoted to each other. Attractive or not, a man who couldn't be faithful held no appeal to me. "It must be hard to be away from her."

He gave me a long look I had trouble interpreting. "We both work a lot so we're used to it."

"What do you do?" I reached for a turkey sandwich as I asked. Did I really want to know more about him? Wouldn't it be better to excuse myself and eat in my room?

"I buy rental properties. That's why I'm here, actually. I'm scoping out the area. And you? What do you do?"

Me? I could lie, but why bother? He belongs to someone, and I should be on a sabbatical from men. "I'm between jobs at the moment." *Did that sound as lame to him as it did to me?*

"We've all been there." He gave me another long look. "Are you here on vacation or considering this area to settle in?"

"Just passing through."

"Heading anywhere interesting?"

There was nothing inappropriate about his questions and he didn't seem to be interested in more than making idle conversation as we ate, but I hesitated and bought time by taking a bite of my sandwich. I searched his face and without thinking it through, asked, "Are you a cop?"

His eyebrows rose. "If I were, would you have anything to hide?"

I coughed on a sip of tea. I didn't have secrets, but I also didn't have much respect for law enforcement. They hadn't protected my parents or me when I'd needed someone to stop the harassment that started once their story went viral. Maybe it wasn't fair to lump the police in with the growing list of people I didn't trust, but if they had an issue with me they'd have to get in line. Outside of Megan, I'd disappointed a good share of those I would have called my friends. They wanted me to snap back to who I was before, but that person had died along with my parents. Whoever I became going forward—there was no going back.

"That was a joke," he said gently, calling my attention to

the fact that I hadn't answered him.

I downed another bite of my sandwich before saying, "Sorry, it's been a long day."

The concern in his eyes was unsettling. "I probably shouldn't bring it up, but I noticed you were upset earlier. Are you okay?"

"Am I okay?" I laughed a little maniacally while tears filled my eyes then gulped down some more tea and fought to remain composed. After releasing a slow breath, I said, "Life has thrown me a few curve balls lately, but as you said, we all go there, right?"

His eyes darkened. "Are you in any danger?"

I sat up straighter. My goal had been to keep things light and social. I was failing to. "No. Nothing like that. Thank you for asking."

My answer didn't appear to appease him. "If you were in any kind of trouble, there are people who would help you, regardless of how messy the situation was."

I rolled my eyes at that. "I'm sure there are. The world is overflowing with heroes."

"Not overflowing, but they're there. All you have to do is ask and one will step up."

My throat tightened with the pain of memories. "I used to believe that, but then I grew up. At the end of the day, even if you're lucky enough to have someone who loves you, you're on your own. The only way to not be disappointed in people is to have zero expectations of anything good coming from them."

God, I hated how I sounded.

I hated even more that this was what I actually believed now.

"Someone hurt you," he said in a low voice.

I blinked back tears again and smiled without humor. "Like you have no idea."

"I'm sorry."

I looked away and shrugged. "I'm the one who should apologize. I bet you didn't think lunch today would be served with a side of woman-who-needs-therapy."

The touch of his hand on the back of mine jolted me, sending my gaze whipping back to meet his. "You're only alone if you choose to be."

I hastily withdrew my hand. "Don't touch me."

He sat back in his chair, watching me like someone trying to solve a puzzle. "Sorry, I come from an affectionate family. I need to remember that not everyone appreciates that."

Feeling confused and defensive, I snapped, "Like your fiancée. I'm sure she'd prefer it if you kept your hands to yourself."

His eyebrows rose again and although I admitted to myself that my reaction to him touching me was more intense than the situation called for, something about him put me on edge. I couldn't explain why I was angry with him or why I didn't simply leave the table.

When my eyes met his again, an unwelcome zing of attraction surged through me and I found yet another reason to mentally flog myself. I had never, not once in my whole life, been tempted by a man who belonged to another. I wasn't a cheater and I'd always told myself I could never want a man who would cheat on a woman.

So, why was I allowing myself, even if it were for just an instant, to lose myself in those beautiful eyes of his? I growled deep in my throat. "It was nice to meet you, Mr. Lamb."

"Evan."

"Mr. Lamb." I stood so abruptly, the chair toppled behind me, hitting the floor with a clatter.

Evan rose to his feet. He seemed about to say something, then changed his mind.

For the second time that day, I turned and fled, not stopping until I was back in my suite. Heart pounding wildly, I leaned against the locked door and gulped in air.

What would my parents say if they were there?

The good thing about having a horrible day is that it makes you appreciate all the good days more.

What do I have to do to start having good days again?

Mom? Dad? You need to send me a freaking guardian angel or a sign or something because I'm not doing so well on my own, and I don't want to be here anymore.

Chapter Four

Everette

AFTER LUNCH, I headed to my room and called Bradford to update him on my progress, or lack thereof. I'd shown a photo of Alexia to several dozen people, but none recognized her. Bradford said he hadn't found any new leads where he was, either. "She might not even be in this area anymore, but someone has to have seen her or the vehicle," Bradford said. "They were here. Traffic cameras caught a silver sedan with state stickers in this area two days ago. Unfortunately, the license plate was shadowed. These people know what they're doing."

"I'll head back out and continue canvassing the area."

"There are several smaller lakes and ponds south of where I am. I'll send you info on the one you should head to tomorrow if neither of us make headway tonight. The longer she's out there, the harder she'll be to find."

"Understood." Even though his voice betrayed little of how he felt, I knew Bradford was worried. The first twenty-four hours held the most hope for retrieval without trauma. He'd warned me each day that passed increased the possibility that we might not bring her home alive. I hadn't faced that situation yet, but he and Cooper had. "We'll find her, Bradford."

"I always do," he said in that cold voice that told me he was thinking what I was.

I cleared my throat. "I need a background check done on a woman I met today."

"You think she's involved?"

I hadn't when I'd first met her, but there was no denying something had and was still traumatizing her. "She might be. I'd like to rule out the possibility."

"You have anything tangible linking her?"

"Just a gut feeling that she's in trouble. If she's involved, she's not a willing participant."

"Good enough for me. What's her name?"

"Shelby Adams. She's the other guest in this bed-and-breakfast."

"I'm running her name through a database now."

"Thanks."

"Mid-twenties?"

"Yes."

"Brunette?"

"Yes." He sent a photo of her to my phone for confirmation. "That's her."

"Nothing posted to social media since . . ."

"Since?"

"Hang on, I'm reading."

After a moment, I said, "I'm trying to be patient, but could you either send me the info or read faster?"

Without missing a beat, Bradford answered, "There's nothing here that implies she'd be linked to a human trafficking ring. Nothing criminal in her background. No warrants. No speeding tickets. She pays her credit cards off in full each month. After a serious tragedy, she moved in with a man named Jeff. He just updated his social media to reflect that he's no longer in a relationship so my guess is they broke up."

"That could explain why she was upset."

"Looks like another dead end."

I had to know. "What was the tragedy?"

"Doesn't matter. Stay focused, Everette. Nothing is more important than locating and retrieving. I'll send you everything you want to know about this Shelby woman after we bring Alexia home."

"When I met Shelby, she was alone and crying. All I want to know is why."

"Is the answer worth Alexia's life?"

"Of course not."

"Then put it out of your head."

"Is it so hard to just fucking tell me what happened to her?"

"Find Alexia, and I'll tell you everything including your new friend's bank balance as well as her favorite color of lipstick. Until then, focus like someone's life depends on it, because it does."

"Understood." Bradford was right. I ended the call, pushed Shelby out of my thoughts, and expanded my circle of search by taking my car. I showed Alexia's photo to someone at every gas station, every store. I showed it to postal workers and landscapers. No one remembered seeing her or the silver sedan.

It was nearly ten by the time I returned to the bed-and-breakfast. Distracted by disappointment, I was caught unaware by Mrs. Allen as I walked across the foyer. "Hungry?"

I shook my head. All day, Bradford's advice had echoed in my thoughts: *Focus like someone's life depends on it, because it does.* Alexia was out there somewhere, possibly being hurt, likely scared, and I had no leads to where she was. What was I missing?

"I'll make you something," Mrs. Allen said in a firm voice. "Come with me."

Tired, I followed her obediently and sat on a barstool at the kitchen's island. She took a glass from a cabinet then opened her refrigerator and filled it with milk. She put two freshly baked chocolate chip cookies on a plate then placed them along with the glass of milk in front of me. "When my sons came home from school with that expression on their faces the only thing that ever made them feel better was a treat."

I let out a slightly amused grunt, but didn't reach for the cookies. "I appreciate the thought, but—"

"Eat them," she ordered.

To appease her, I took a bite of the most heavenly cookie I'd ever tasted outside of my mother's. The milk was a perfect chaser. "Not bad," I said with a tired wink.

She rested her elbows on the other side of the island and

looked me in the eye. "It's none of my business, but you don't look like a happily engaged man."

Reminding myself that Alexia was all that mattered, I said, "Appearances can be deceiving."

"What are you really doing here, Evan Lamb? And why do I think it's not to check out rental properties?"

I stiffened. Okay, so I hadn't mastered the art of subterfuge yet. I looked her over for any hint that she might be the type to be involved in human trafficking. Bradford said I had good instincts when it came to people. He didn't say anything he didn't mean. So, what was my gut telling me about this older woman? Beyond how weird it was that she seemed to find me attractive, there was nothing that stood out. I decided to test that theory. If she was involved at all, there'd be some hint of it in her eyes when I showed her Alexia's photo. "Actually, I'm looking for someone. The daughter of a friend of mine." I brought up a picture of Alexia on my phone and showed it to Mrs. Allen. "Have you seen her?"

To give her credit, Mrs. Allen studied the photo intently before shaking her head. "Sorry, no, but I don't get out much. She looks young. Is she a runaway?"

"Something like that." *Follow your instincts.* "I'm leaving tomorrow morning to look for her south of here. If you see her, will you contact me?"

"Absolutely." Pursing her lips, Mrs. Allen straightened. "Her parents must be frantic."

"They are."

She looked me over again. "You're a good man to help them locate her."

My shoulders slumped. "I just hope we find her."

Mrs. Allen poured herself a glass of water, sipped it, then said, "I'm surprised your fiancée isn't here searching with you."

When I didn't say anything, she added, "You don't have one, do you?"

I downed the second cookie, asking myself how Bradford would have handled Mrs. Allen. "Why would I lie about that?"

Her hand came to her mouth as she seemed to ponder that. "I am an avid reader. Mysteries mostly. If I had to guess, I'd say it's part of your cover story and that your name isn't even Evan Lamb."

Wiping a crumb of cookie from the corner of my mouth, I said, "Imagine what that would say about me if it were true. I'd either be a pathological liar or a horrible spy. Do I look like either one of those?" I shot her a charm-filled smile that brought an answering smile to her face.

"No, I suppose not," she said with a sigh. "You're far too handsome to be either."

I chuckled at that. "I don't believe one determines the other, but I'll accept the compliment as long as it comes with another cookie."

She placed another on my plate. "Are you a love 'em and leave 'em type?"

"No, ma'am. I've spent my whole life in the same small town and my mother would whip my ass if I broke the hearts of any of her friends' daughters."

Mrs. Allen laughed at that. "Is that where your fiancée is

from?"

"I don't have—"

"Knew it."

I clapped a hand to my forehead and muttered, "Mrs. Allen, what was your profession before you opened a bed-and-breakfast?"

"School psychologist. I can sniff out a lie from a mile away."

I lowered my hand and nodded slowly. "Yes, you can."

Her expression turned serious. "I also know how hard it is all around when a child runs away. Is there anything I can do to help?"

Could I trust her? Considering how little else we had to go on, I decided it was worth the risk. "We think she was lured away by a man driving a silver sedan with state stickers on the back window of the vehicle. He goes by Curtis, but there's no way to know if that's his real name. The more time that goes by without finding her—"

"You don't have to say it. I know. I'll make a few calls."

"There's something else. His family might own a lake house."

"That's not much to go on since that could be anyone in the area."

"Sandy?" Shelby said tentatively as she stepped into the kitchen. "Oh, I'm sorry. I slept through dinner and thought—I can wait until breakfast."

"Get on in here. I put aside a plate for you. It'll take but a moment to heat up." Mrs. Allen waved for Shelby to join us.

"You don't have to—"

"Sit yourself down," Mrs. Allen said while pulling a plate of chicken and vegetables out of the refrigerator.

For a moment, Shelby hovered at the doorway before making her way over and sitting on the farthest barstool from me. "Thank you. If it's okay, I'll take it to my room."

With the microwave humming behind her, Mrs. Allen looked from me to Shelby and back. "Have you asked *her*?"

I shook my head.

"Asked me what?" Shelby's expression was guarded.

"*Evan . . .*" Mrs. Allen said my name slowly and with emphasis as if expecting me to correct her before adding, "isn't here scoping out rental properties. He's actually looking for a young woman who may or may not have been lured away by a man for nefarious reasons. Show her the photo, Evan."

I brought the photo of Alexia up on my phone then turned it toward her. "Have you seen her?"

"No, sorry," Shelby answered and my hand clenched on my phone. I'd spent all day trying to keep Shelby out of my thoughts, but she kept creeping back in. The circles under her eyes were a testament to how whatever tragedy she'd suffered was still haunting her, but I couldn't let her be the reason I didn't find Alexia. Whatever she'd been through, whatever she was going through, would have to wait.

I repocketed my phone. "I'll leave my information with Mrs. Allen. If you do see her, please contact me. Her family is suffering. It's vital that we find Alexia before something happens to her."

Shelby stared down at the plate of food Mrs. Allen had placed in front of her. She was quiet for long enough that I stood and prepared to leave her to eat in peace.

Just as I was about to thank Mrs. Allen for the cookies, Shelby raised her eyes to mine. "It might be nothing, but when I was by the lake . . ."

"Yes?" I held my breath.

"My memory lately hasn't been as good as it once was . . ."

I growled in frustration. "What did you see?"

"Nothing. I saw nothing, but I did hear a conversation this morning when I was sitting by the lake. The female voice sounded young and there was a man with her . . ."

"What did you hear?" I tried but failed to contain my impatience.

"Let her remember," Mrs. Allen said firmly.

I sighed. "Sorry. Take your time, Shelby. And don't leave anything out, even if you think it's not important. It might be."

Clasping her hands on the table, Shelby inhaled visibly and nodded. "She asked how long they had to stay here before they would head down to New York City. She sounded excited about going with him. He said the wait would be worth it. I wasn't really listening to them, but I think he said he was setting up appointments with agents for her and they needed to wait one more day."

Goose bumps. I had fucking goose bumps as her words sunk in. "That was her. It has to be. Are you sure they said New York?"

"I'm pretty sure." She frowned. "Yes, I'm positive. It was New York."

"Do you know which way they were walking?"

Her eyes widened and she went pale. "I didn't—I'm not—you know the direction you came from? I think they came that way and walked past me in the other direction. At least, that's how it sounded."

Overcome with emotion, I walked over to Shelby and took both of her hands in mine. They were cold and shaking. "You may have just saved a life."

Her eyes filled with tears. "That would sure be a sign that I'm still here for a reason, wouldn't it?"

I hated whoever had hurt her and knew this would be far from the last time I saw her. Adrenaline pumping through me, my hands tightened on hers and I vowed, "I'm going to find Alexia and then I'm coming back for you."

A myriad of emotions gave her several comical expressions. Her mouth opened and closed without sound, like a fish trying to breathe out of water.

I followed my heart and kissed her, boldly but briefly, then released her hands and took out my phone again. "I have to go, but take care of her for me, Mrs. Allen."

"I will," Mrs. Allen said vehemently.

There was no time to ask myself if I'd crossed boundaries or been too spontaneous. I was on the phone before I made it out of the kitchen. "Bradford, I have a lead."

Behind me, I heard Shelby breathlessly ask, "What just happened?"

Chapter Five

Shelby

HAND COVERING MY mouth, I fought to quiet the storm within me. Mr. Gorgeous-But-Engaged had just kissed me like a lead man in a movie leaving for battle, and Mrs. Allen didn't appear to see anything wrong with that. Shell-shocked, I slowly pushed the stool back from the island and stood.

Fanning her face with a napkin, she said, "That made me want to meet my husband for the first time all over again."

I swayed on my feet. "Thank you for dinner, but I'm not hungry anymore."

Turning her attention to me, Mrs. Allen's expression was sympathetic. "He's not engaged, you know. He is one hundred percent single, small-town raised, and still fears his mama. You don't let one like that get away."

I shook my head. "Wait, he told you that?"

"Sure did."

"And you believe him?"

Her head tilted to one side and her hands went to her hips. "He's running off to save a young girl. Yes, I believe him."

It might have been because it was late and I'd woken from a nap that had left me feeling more tired than better, but I was struggling to process what had just happened. "If he lied about being engaged, how do you know he didn't lie about being single? Or about any of the rest of this? We don't know him. He could be tracking that girl to kill her for all we know. And I just gave him her location." The possibility sent a shudder down my back.

Considering my recent run of luck, it was a more likely scenario. I hugged my arms around my waist as a wave of nausea hit me.

"Is that what you see when you look at him? A killer?" she asked.

"I don't know what I see in anyone anymore." That was the raw truth.

Mrs. Allen sat down on a stool. "Want to talk about it?"

"Not really."

She nodded toward the seat I'd vacated. "Sometimes the best person to share your thoughts with is someone who isn't involved. They can see things clearly when someone in the thick of things can't."

I shook my head. "I'm done looking back. I need to move forward."

She gave me a long look. "What's her name?"

"Who?"

"Your best friend. The one who told you about my place."

How did she know that? "Megan."

"She called to make sure I had a vacancy."

"She's a good friend."

"She also left her number and asked me to contact her if you seemed—sad."

My cheeks warmed with shame and I looked away. "I'm fine."

"It's okay to not be. You've been through a lot."

I stiffened at that. "What did Megan tell you?"

"Just your name, but I don't let people I haven't checked out stay here. My husband used to do cyber security. I know how to scan someone's socials. That's how I knew Evan Lamb wasn't being honest about who he was and that you were sent to me for a reason."

"No, I came here by chance. I was driving without a destination in mind. There was no way for Megan to know where I'd end up."

"I didn't say your friend sent you. Did you ever consider that people land where they're supposed to?"

"No." Anger rose within me. "The thought that anything I've been through was by design would make me physically sick."

She nodded. "I understand. I lost a son to a freak accident. He was home from college and I was so damn proud of him. He was the kind of person who lit every room he walked into. When he told me he and his local friends were gathering for a softball game in a field down the street, just like they had in high school—I imagined them coming here afterward, trashing my kitchen, eating everything in sight. They never did. He was running backward for a fly ball, tripped, and hit his head on a rock wall. I wasn't prepared to lose him. I wanted someone to blame and hated everyone for longer than I care to admit. Even my husband and my other son. I felt that they should have done something. Saved him, somehow. I don't know. I took an early retirement and sat in this house wondering why it hadn't been me instead of him. Parents aren't supposed to outlive their children. Then someone needed a place to stay and we rented them a room; it felt like the right thing to do. Even though I had my husband, it was nice to have someone else around. So we kept renting out rooms. I'm not going to claim I understand how the universe works, but when I needed something to wake up and get out of bed for, that's what I was sent. I don't believe my son died for a reason, but I do believe we don't carry the weight of what happens to us on our own. Maybe that's something I have to believe or I'd go insane, but it's comforted me through some rough times. And I could be choosing a fantasy over reality, but my heart tells me you came here because you needed to meet someone who also knows what it's like to lose someone they love and not know how to go on without them."

It was a lot—too much. I couldn't accept it, so I didn't. I turned, walked away, and made it all the way to my room before I let a tear spill over. I grabbed my luggage and started throwing clothing into it, then stopped and sat on the bed beside it.

I wanted to run, but to where?

What was out there waiting for me?

I'd asked my parents for a sign—what if all of this was

exactly that?

What if I allowed myself to imagine that they were still with me, watching over me, offering to share the weight of what had happened to us? Would that change how meaningless everything had felt since I'd lost them?

Did I dare believe I could have played even the smallest role in saving a young girl's life? And that Evan, if that was even his name, had meant anything he'd said?

What kind of man kisses a woman he doesn't know and promises to come back for her? That alone should have been enough to convince me he was either a player or as in need of mental health services as I was.

Imagine how naïve a person would have to be to believe a man like that would want to settle down with one woman. Or that he was on a heroic quest.

And Mrs. Allen?

If she didn't already hate me for walking away when she'd offered me only a warm meal and kindness—why would she want someone like me hanging around? Wouldn't I just remind her of what she'd lost?

She said her beliefs brought her comfort.

Nothing had done that for me so far. Not Megan, no matter how good of a friend she'd been. Not Jeff, even though he'd given it a good try. Staying hadn't felt right. Leaving hadn't solved anything.

Should I drink whatever Kool-Aid Mrs. Allen had?

Okay, so sometimes shit went down and it sucked.

And I'm human so I didn't continue on like a machine. I fucked things up then fucked them up again. There was also a very good chance I wasn't done fucking things up.

But maybe my parents sent me here.

Maybe Mrs. Allen did understand, and I needed to talk to someone like that.

And Mr. I'll-be-back-for-you?

I wasn't ready for him, but if people really did land where they were supposed to, he wouldn't come back until I was.

I stood, carefully unpacked my clothing again, and decided to give Mrs. Allen and her view of the world a chance. A little while later, I returned to the kitchen and found her still there, this time with a plate of fresh cookies and two glasses of milk.

"I knew you'd come back," she said, pushing the treats across the island toward me. "Would you like to try a homemade cookie? They always brought a smile to my sons' faces. They're also grandchild approved."

I accepted the plate and sat down across from her. "You have grandchildren?"

"Two. They're in middle school now. Smart, but so mouthy to their parents. They don't pull any of that when they're here."

Remembering something Evan had said, I joked, "Or they'd catch the spoon."

She laughed. "You know it. I'd never actually hit them, but they don't know that. It's enough for them to simply believe I would."

I picked up a cookie and kept my gaze on it rather than her when I said, "Thank you for—everything. I am struggling and do need someone to talk to."

Holding up her glass of milk, she said, "Then let's make a toast to new friendships."

I raised my glass to clink with hers. "To new friendships."

"And hot men with bulging biceps."

I laughed then nodded. "And hot men with bulging biceps."

We both drank to that and for the first time in what seemed like forever I didn't feel alone.

Chapter Six

Everette

A FEW DAYS later, seated at our usual table at Little Willie's in Driverton, my friends and I gathered to celebrate my return to town. In the past, Cooper had come back from a "job" more than a little beaten up. It could have been my imagination, but both Ollie and Levi seemed a little disappointed that I was unscathed.

Katie, Ollie's cousin and his only reliable waitress, took her time coming over. She and Levi had always been good friends, but lately things seemed strained between them. When she came to our table, she greeted me with a huge smile. "What does our newest town hero want today? It's on the house."

"Hey," Ollie said. "Easy on the freebie offers, Katie. He can afford to pay."

She rolled her eyes at her cousin then beamed another smile at me. "Tom told me you found that girl and brought her home safely."

"I didn't do it on my own. All I did was help locate her and get her back to her family. Bradford handled the . . .

complicated parts."

Katie tucked her serving tray beneath her arm. "That sounds like a lot to me. We're all crazy proud of you. Your family was here for breakfast and we decided to name a special after you. What do you think of Everette's Beefed-Up Burger?"

Knowing it would get a laugh from her, I raised an arm and flexed. "Make it a double patty."

"Done," she said with a chuckle.

Levi muttered, "Make it a double patty."

I did what any good friend would and slugged him so hard in the arm he winced. "Bradford is willing to beef you up as well. All you have to do is put down the beer and pick up some weights."

"I'm happy the way I am," he said before punching me back. When his fist connected, he swore then shook his hand. "What the fuck did you do to your arms—install steel?"

Ollie leaned forward and poked me in the chest. "Seriously, I see you every day. How did I not notice you were bulking up? You're not taking that stuff that will give you the name of my bar, are you?"

"Sure am. I didn't want you to be the only one with that condition," I joked with a smirk and a wink at Katie. We'd all grown up together and she was not only like a sister to us, but we treated her like one of the guys.

With an amused sigh, Katie asked us what we wanted. When I ordered a water, Levi mocked, "Bradford has you grounded like you missed curfew in high school. Can you honestly tell me it's worth it?"

Rather than answering lightly, I chose what they needed to hear—honesty. "It wasn't easy and it's tempting as hell to order a few rounds of shots and sit here laughing the afternoon away, but I feel good about the changes I've made. It's not about how I look or impressing anyone. I'm sleeping better, am healthier, and I no longer feel—small. And I'm not talking about physically. You guys know me better than anyone. I love it here, but there have been times I've felt trapped, too. I don't feel that way anymore. I can support my family, be here with you, and still do something for myself. That's what Bradford gave me—something for me. When I called Alexia's parents and told them she was safe and on her way back to them . . . there is no moonshine, not even yours, Levi, that gives a better high than that feeling. I know things won't always go as well and I'll fail sometimes at this, but I can't go back to simply coasting through life and wishing things were better."

Katie hugged her tray to her. "Cooper offered to pay for college for me. I didn't accept. I want to go so why do I keep saying no? What am I so afraid of?"

"Failing," I said gently. "And that's normal."

Levi cleared his throat. "Bradford said he could help me sell my moonshine recipe. He also offered to put me through his boot camp if I give up drinking."

"I own a bar," Ollie said. "What kind of bar owner doesn't drink?"

"A successful one?" Katie said in a soft tone. "Maybe we *are* meant for more. I've always been fascinated by forensic science. My grades in high school were good. I wonder if Bradford has room in his boot camp for women as well."

"I'm sure he does," I said with confidence.

Levi gave Katie a long look. "You're interested?"

She nodded.

"If you do it," he said, "I'll do it."

"Really?" The smile she shot him lit up her face. "We could help keep each other motivated."

He nodded. "I've been doing some thinking lately and I can see why Mary was never interested in me. It's time to get my life together. Who knows, if I do, maybe she'll give me another shot."

Ollie spoke over whatever Katie might have been about to say. He said, "If you're all in, I guess I have no choice but to do it as well. It'd be no damn fun to drink on my own."

I clapped a hand on his back. "It's not that bad, I promise. I start every day with a run now. It's something we could all do together."

"Oh, my fucking God." Ollie ran his hand through his hair. "You're serious."

Katie looked around the table and said, "So, not the usual round of drinks today?"

"I'll have a water and the Everette's Beefed-Up Burger," I said with an attempt at a straight face.

Without missing a beat, Levi added, "I'll have a ginger ale and a *Levi Will Punch Everette in his Face if his Ego Gets any Bigger* with a side of fries."

"With or without pickles?" Katie asked with a twinkle in her eyes.

"Extra pickles," he answered. "I might need some as ammunition."

Smiling, Ollie said, "Bring me a roast beef please with a coffee and a bowl of *This Will Probably Kill Me*, but I guess I'm in."

Katie was laughing as she walked away. She returned a moment later with our drinks then left us again to wait on her other customers. In a town like Driverton, there wasn't anyone we didn't know and people didn't come to Little Willie's for quick service. It was the only place to eat in town outside of Manju's Donuts.

Ollie updated me on the town's gossip, but it was nothing outside the norm. Someone's dog was bothering someone's chickens again. Some teenagers were caught partying down by Mrs. Tissbury's pond. She called Ollie's mother who gave them all a stern talking to and had them over at her house the next day to not just pick up their trash but also mow Mrs. Tissbury's lawn and weed her garden. Mrs. Williams was a force to be reckoned with. Had they refused, she would have had their parents out there cleaning up as well. No one wanted to be the child of someone Mrs. Williams lectured into picking up after them. It was good to know that regardless of how much was changing about Driverton, all the important things were staying the same.

Levi said Pete Glenford had come over to help him give his tractor a tune-up. "He's gearing up to be a grandfather. It's good to see Dotty and him so happy."

It was. When our conversation lulled, I leaned back in my seat and asked, "Did I tell you about the woman I met while I was in Rhode Island?"

"You didn't." Ollie's eyes narrowed. "If you say you're moving away to be with her, I'll kick your ass and rename your burger *Never Forget the Time Everette Pissed His Pants in Kindergarten.*"

I laugh/groaned. "I'm not moving anywhere and Katie would never let you do that."

He made a face across the bar at his cousin. "You're right. She's a killjoy."

"Hey," Levi said, "Katie is the best thing about this town and you know it."

That snapped Ollie's attention back to Levi. "Don't fuck my cousin."

Levi's face went red. "You know, one day you're going to make a joke about her that I'm going to cram down your throat with my fist."

Even my eyes widened at that. "Guys? Chill. Anything going on that I should know about?"

Still looking flustered, Levi said, "Ollie's being an asshole again. Katie got her hair cut yesterday and I told her she looked pretty. I was being nice. He's been a dick about it since."

Ollie leaned over until he was eye to eye with Levi. "I couldn't love you more if you were blood related to me, Levi, but I've seen your sorry ass when it comes to dating. You suck at it. Cats are more loyal than you are. Stay the fuck away from Katie."

Levi raised a hand. "First, no one at this table has a good track record when it comes to relationships, so your opinion doesn't carry weight. Second, Katie isn't a child anymore. If she ever wanted to be with me there wouldn't be a damn thing you could do about it. And third," he mirrored Ollie's posturing, "I'm pretty sure I could thumb wrestle you to the ground, but do you need me to prove it?"

I coughed on a laugh.

Ollie growled, then laughed and sat back. "No, you have the thumbs of an ape. But seriously, Katie is off-limits."

Levi threw his hands up in the air. "You don't think I know that? She and I are friends, Ollie. Friends. That's not off-limits too, is it?"

Deciding my topic was safer, I interjected, "So her name is Shelby Adams. A few months ago, both of her parents died in a fire during a home invasion."

"Holy shit," Ollie said.

"Did they catch the guy?" Levi asked.

"He died in the fire as well." When neither of them said anything, I added, "She's still struggling with it."

"No kidding." Ollie's sarcasm didn't mean he didn't care. It was his go-to mode when he wasn't sure how to respond.

"Man," Levi said, "I can't imagine what I'd do."

Ollie tilted his head in question. "Did she ask for help finding someone else who was involved?"

"No. She was just the other guest at a bed-and-breakfast I stayed at."

"Okay." Ollie shot Levi a confused look. "Outside of how sad what happened to her is, why do we care?"

In a low voice, I mumbled, "I told her I'd go back for her."

Levi leaned forward. "What was that? What did you say?"

"I think he said he said he'd go back for her." Ollie shook his head.

I gulped down half of my glass of water while I asked myself if mentioning Shelby to my friends had been a bad move. There was no one I trusted more or who'd seen me both at my best and worst and stayed with me through it all. I needed their opinion on what my next step should be. "When I met her she was crying. I didn't know why, but I knew I wanted to help her. At the time, Alexia was my priority so I couldn't. Shelby had overheard a conversation between Alexia and the man who was planning to hand her off to someone in New York. It was that tip that gave us what we needed to narrow our search and find Alexia. I knew that as soon as I heard it and I was so grateful I said I'd return after Alexia was safe. I said it in the heat of the moment and now I don't know what to do."

"Oh, no," Ollie said with mock dread. "You're starting to believe you really are a hero."

Levi put a cloth napkin over his head like a bonnet and batted his eyes at me. "I'm just a damsel in distress waiting for some big, strong man to rescue me. Help me, Everette."

"We were out of what you ordered, Levi," Katie said cheerfully, "so I brought you a plate of *I Hope Your Voice Doesn't Stay That Way*."

In his rush to get the napkin off his head, he nearly knocked the tray from her hands. I barked out a laugh that Ollie echoed.

As she handed us our food, Katie asked, "What are they giving you shit about now, Everette?"

"Don't blame them, Katie. I shouldn't have brought it up. I don't know why I thought they'd be able to help me."

She pulled up a chair and joined us. "Okay, now I'm curious. Ignore these idiots. You obviously need a woman's advice." She side-eyed Levi. "So pipe down, Princess."

Looking unoffended, Levi shrugged off her comment and said, "Fine. He's all yours. Let's see if you can hear what he did and not mock him."

Katie turned those sweet eyes of hers back to me. "What did you do, Everette?"

I reluctantly repeated what I'd just told Ollie and Levi.

Frowning, Katie asked, "Wait, she gave you a clue and you promised to come back for her and just left?"

I made a face. "I might have kissed her right before I told her I'd come back for her."

The expression on Katie's face was the same one she used to look at newborn puppies. "That is so adorable and probably the most romantic thing I've ever heard."

"He's lucky she didn't call the cops," Ollie said. "Men can't just walk up to women and kiss them like that."

Katie shrugged. "When they look like Everette they can."

Levi growled some profanity under his breath, and I gave him a look. If he really was sweet on Katie, I didn't want to be around when Ollie found out.

I rubbed a hand down my face. "I was hyped up because I knew Shelby had just given us what we'd been afraid we wouldn't find. Bradford accessed the highway cameras and they'd barely pulled out of town the next morning before we had them. There was a lot to do after that. I didn't have time to go back to the bed-and-breakfast. Now I want to, but she's probably gone. And if she's not, what the hell would I say to her? I met her as Evan Lamb. She thinks I have a fiancée. That was all part of my alias. It's crazy to think about reaching out to her, right?"

"A little," Katie said in a serious tone. A heavy silence followed until she added, "The Everette I used to know would have let that stop him. But you're not that man anymore, are you? You're no longer okay with sitting back and hoping the world becomes a better place. You're out there making a difference. So, maybe it's not crazy. Maybe you shouldn't let what any of us think stop you from keeping the promise you made to her."

"That's actually good advice," Levi said.

"If you end up married to this woman," Ollie said, "she moves here. I've invested too much into our friendship to not miss you if you leave."

Katie humorously dabbed at the corners of her eyes. "Ollie, that's the sweetest thing I've ever heard you say."

"I'm not looking to date her," I said forcefully. When none of them appeared to believe me, I added, "I just want to help her."

"Help her," Levi joked. "Is that what they call bumping the uglies now?"

Katie laughed, "Levi, if your bits and pieces are ugly that's nothing to brag about."

Ollie cut in. "I'm with Katie." He waved at Levi as if he

was a lost cause. "Not about you. Everette, it wouldn't hurt to call her."

I was torn. "Levi, you were right earlier when you said none of us have ever been good at relationships. I might look different on the outside, but I'm still figuring the inside shit out." I hated to say it aloud, but I did. "I still live with my parents."

"Because you pay their mortgage and you're putting your siblings through college, not because you're a deadbeat. Anyone who judges you for that doesn't have their priorities straight," Levi said with more emotion than I expected from him.

"Thanks." We gave each other shit on the regular, but his opinion meant a lot to me.

"I have an idea," Ollie said. "Since we're all enrolling in Bradford's school for sobriety and success, why don't you ask him?"

"I don't hate that idea," Katie said.

"Do it," Levi encouraged. "He seems to know what he's talking about." Waving a finger in the air, he added, "and he's the one who'd bail you out if you get arrested for harassment."

"Nice," I said with sarcasm, but took out my phone. "I hate to bother him with something like this, but he did tell me I could call him anytime." Plus it was easier to call him than Shelby so I did.

"Speak," Bradford said gruffly.

"Do you have a moment to give me an opinion on a situation?"

"I wouldn't have answered if I didn't."

I put him on speakerphone. The sound of gunfire took all of us by surprise. In a rush, I said, "If you're busy, I can call back."

Another shot was fired in the distance. "Just be quick. What do you need?"

Levi asked, "Is he in the middle of a firefight?"

"That's a forty-five. Holy shit, don't get him killed, Everette. Tell him about Shelby later," Ollie said.

"Hold on," Bradford growled. "Do you honestly believe I'd answer the phone if I was dodging bullets?"

None of us denied it because we all had pretty much thought he would.

He sighed. "Everette, your training is not complete if that entered your head as a possibility. People who lose focus end up dead—don't forget that."

"I know."

Sounding a little amused, Bradford said, "I'll take it as a compliment that you all think I'm badass enough to do that, but that only happens in the movies. You keep your head down and your mouth shut if you want to live when the bullets start flying."

"I'll remember that," I said, feeling that it might not be the right time to ask him for advice about Shelby. "Hey, Ollie, Levi, and Katie were just saying they want to train with you now."

"That's the situation you want my opinion on?"

"No?"

"Yes or no? Which is it?"

"It's no. Okay, I'm going to just tell you."

"That would make this conversation go a hell of a lot easier."

"Remember that woman Shelby . . ." At the prompting of Katie, I spilled the whole story to him then waited.

He didn't say anything at first. "You guys aren't drinking, are you?"

"Nope, this is a completely embarrassing yet sober call."

After a moment, he said, "Her story really touched you."

"It did."

"Then why are you in Driverton?"

One by one I met the eyes of my closest friends while I admitted the truth. "I'm not a hero, Bradford. I'm just a man doing the best he can for his family and trying to make a difference. I don't know anything about helping someone through a trauma."

Katie put her hand over mine and gave me a supportive smile. "You'll figure it out."

Levi nodded. "I've never met anyone nicer than you, Everette."

"Me neither," Ollie added. "And for the record, Everette, promising Shelby you'd go back for her? That's kind of badass. You should get an extra star or stripe on your Bradford Academy uniform or something."

Bradford laughed. "Ollie, you sure you want to play with me?"

With surprising sincerity, Ollie said, "We're glad you're here, Bradford. And we actually value your opinion, which is why we called you."

In a gruff voice, Bradford asked, "Everette, what do you need to make this happen?"

I hadn't put a lot of thought into it because I hadn't allowed myself to imagine actually going back down to Rhode Island for Shelby. "I'd need someone to check in on my family."

"Done," Levi and Ollie said.

"I have a carving started, but—"

"I'll finish it," Bradford said.

I winced, but said, "Thanks. And then I need a plan for what to say to her when I get there."

"We can figure that out," Ollie said with confidence then turned to his cousin. "We'll just need a round of—" He stopped when I shook my head, then said, "soda." He made a face.

I clapped a hand on his shoulder. "It gets easier, Ollie. A month from now you'll be thanking me."

"You'd better be right," he grumbled.

"I am," I said with confidence. "Now, back to Shelby. Should I call first? Apologize or show up and act like nothing happened?"

Chapter Seven

Shelby

FROM MY FAVORITE spot on Mrs. Allen's porch stairs, I paused my typing to look out over the water. With her help, I'd tweaked my résumé and was in the process of sending it to several companies that offered remote work. I wasn't ready to return to my old job or even an office, something I'd been beating myself up about for months. Mrs. Allen was helping me focus less on who I thought I should be and more on who I was.

Instead of starting the day listing everything I didn't like about myself, she encouraged me to start a gratitude journal. The goal was to write not only what I was grateful for, but also what I'd like to be grateful for. I'll admit I'd initially struggled to fill a page on the first day. I was incredibly grateful for her as well as Megan. Other than them? Most things I thought about made me either sad or angry.

I was physically healthy, though.

The sound of birds in the morning was a better wake-up call than an alarm.

I was grateful for the college degree my parents had

pushed me to acquire because it would make it easier for me to find a job I might actually enjoy. Education equaled options. At least, that's what my mother had always said.

I was grateful for the years I'd had with my parents and all the love they'd shown me. The best parts of me were there because they'd modeled being respectful, decent, and kind. Not everyone could say that about the people who'd raised them.

I was grateful that my last job had allowed me to save the money I was currently surviving on. It wouldn't last forever, but if I was careful, it would buy me time to figure out what I wanted to do next.

It took a few days, but I added Jeff to what I was grateful for. No, we hadn't been a love match, but he'd taken me in when I'd needed to hide from the world and he'd kicked me out when I was strong enough to survive on my own. I sent him a short text, which I'd like to think expressed that to him. He didn't answer, but as I began to see things more clearly I understood why. When I'd said we hadn't been a love match, I'd still been focused on myself and my experience. I almost went down the rabbit hole of being ashamed of how I'd treated Jeff, but Mrs. Allen helped me see that there was no benefit to that path. I couldn't go back and change what I'd done. I couldn't change that I didn't love him. All I could do was be grateful for how good he'd been to me and be better going forward.

Speaking of moving forward, there was one kiss that kept haunting me and it hadn't been from Jeff. No, the kiss that lingered in my thoughts and I kept reliving in my dreams had been delivered with an empty promise from someone I'd likely never see again.

I need to forget him.

He's not coming back.

And I don't want him to.

I don't need a man to save me. I'm doing better every day.

I turned to greet Mr. Allen as he came out onto the porch. "How's the job search going?"

I closed my laptop and placed it beside me. "Still sending out résumés, but I'm feeling hopeful that I'll find something soon."

"Sandy and I were talking this morning. If you're considering staying through the weekend, we'd like to lower the rate you're paying."

I blinked back tears and turned to face the water so he wouldn't see how deeply their kindness affected me. "That's not necessary. I should be paying extra. Your wife has helped me more than she'll probably ever know."

"Don't underestimate how much you being here means to her as well. We all forget to follow our own best advice now and then. This has been good for her."

I swallowed hard. "I'm glad. If my friend Megan ever hits a rough spot, I know where to send her. I feel like I've been at a motivational retreat."

"My only complaint is she baked so many cookies this week I've put on five pounds."

I glanced back at him and laughed. "Me too."

Mr. Allen's expression hardened, his eyes narrowed and he rose to his full height. "What is he doing back here?"

The door behind him opened and shut. Mrs. Allen asked, "Drew, what's wrong?"

"Maybe nothing, maybe something. Wait here, I'll be right back."

I rose to my feet as he strode past me. It was only then that I spotted who he had—the man who'd claimed to be Evan Lamb. I rushed down a step to stop Mr. Allen from confronting him. If there was trouble, I'd have a better chance fending off someone than a man in his late sixties. A myriad of horrible scenarios flashed through my head as well as a wave of guilt that I hadn't been there when my parents needed me. I knew in that instant that I was capable of putting aside my fear and choosing violence.

"Shelby, don't," Mrs. Allen said in a firm voice that stopped me in my tracks. "Drew's a proud man and he wants to protect you. Don't take that from him."

It took me a moment to process what she was saying. My emotions were still so close to the surface that they sometimes rose up and nearly consumed me. I clenched my hands at my sides and took a deep breath as Mr. Allen stepped in front of Evan, blocking his approach. They exchanged words I couldn't make out.

From beside me, Mrs. Allen made a satisfied cluck. "He said he'd come back and he did. I like a man who keeps his word."

The optimism in her voice was in stark contrast to the churning nervousness in mine. "Too bad we don't know his name or how much of what he told us is true."

Mrs. Allen stepped close to me. "Drew is a good judge of

character. I guarantee he won't let Evan past him if he doesn't think it's safe."

I watched with fascination as Evan handed Mr. Allen his wallet, then his phone. "What are they doing?"

Mrs. Allen said, "Looks like Drew is grilling him and demanding proof of whatever he is saying."

Mr. Allen looked down at Evan's phone, seemed to swipe through it, then said something to Evan that he agreed to. With Evan's phone to his ear, Mr. Allen's voice carried all the way to us. "Hello, my name is Drew Allen. I have your son here. Do you mind if I ask you a few questions?"

My hand flew to my mouth. "No. Do you really think he's talking to Evan's parents?"

"Drew doesn't have patience for liars. He doesn't like that Evan came here under false pretenses, but is willing to give him one more chance if he did it for the reason he said."

"Wow." My initial impression of Mr. Allen had been completely off. I'd thought he was quiet and shy, but there was nothing shy about him. Despite being a foot or so shorter than Evan, he was commanding respect. I glimpsed what Mrs. Allen had fallen for. My father would have given his life to protect my mother and me. It's why I never believed for a second that he'd set the fire. His first priority would have been to protect my mother and get her out of there.

After handing the phone back to Evan, he continued to talk to him. Evan nodded in agreement to whatever he was saying.

You go, Mr. Allen.

The two shook hands then began to walk toward us. My breath caught in my throat when my gaze locked with Evan's. He was gorgeous by any woman's definition, but when he smiled I rocked back onto my heels and steadied myself by holding on to the railing.

"Now that," Mrs. Allen said, "is how Drew looks at me whenever he comes back from a trip. I hate to miss him, but I do love how he comes home to me."

"He's probably back for something he forgot—a charger or something."

"Sure. Keep telling yourself that."

With Mr. Allen at his side, Evan stopped at the bottom of the steps. The intensity of his gaze warmed me from head to toe. "Hi."

"Hi," I answered. It wasn't witty, but I was having difficulty thinking while his attention was focused on me.

Mr. Allen said, "I'd like to introduce both of you to Everette Morin. According to his father, he's calm-natured, honest, *not* engaged, and hard-working."

The pink flush Mr. Allen's words elicited on Evan's—no, *Everette's* cheeks—was the sweetest thing I'd ever seen. "That's quite an endorsement."

Everette shrugged. "He's my dad, he's supposed to think highly of me."

That wasn't always the case, but I loved that Everette thought it was. I also didn't mind hearing he was single. No, I didn't mind hearing that at all. "Why are you here?"

He glanced at our older chaperones, both of whom were making no secret of their interest, then said, "I thought you might—I had an idea that—are you looking for a job?"

A wave of disappointment rushed through me. For just a moment I'd let myself imagine he'd found it impossible to forget me and had come back to . . . what? What could he have offered that I would have said yes to?

To sweep me off my feet and take me somewhere? Away from all my problems? I would have refused. Been there, done that.

To date me? I wasn't ready to start anything new with anyone.

So, why had his reason for coming back left me feeling deflated?

"What makes you think I'd be interested in whatever position you're offering?" I asked in a huskier voice than I'd intended.

"Because you have a pulse," Mrs. Allen said beneath her breath. Her husband shook his head at her and she laughed. "Sorry, but it's true. He wouldn't have trouble hiring someone to pick up dog poo from his front yard."

A quick glance at Mr. Allen revealed that he was amused rather than annoyed by his wife's antics. My father would have been as well. Flirtatious jokes held no weight when a partnership was secure. I used to think I was destined to find someone who'd love me that way, but my confidence had been shaken as well. If life had a playbook, it was one that didn't make any damn sense to me.

"I do have two dogs. My family does, anyway. A Chihuahua named JJ and a beagle named Penny. My mother takes care of them most of the time, but if you ever want to help hunt down the tiny messes they make in the yard . . ." There was a twinkle in Everette's eyes as he spoke.

"Tempting as that sounds, I'll pass."

Everette hooked his thumbs in the front pockets of his jeans. "Looks like you were wrong, Mrs. Allen. Thankfully that wasn't the job I'm hiring for."

Was it my imagination or was the temperature rising? "I'm only interested in remote work at this time."

"That's a shame," he said smoothly. "Although probably for the best. It's not a job that pays much."

A smile pulled my lips. "You're not selling it well."

"And the training for it is extensive." I cocked my head to one side. As the embarrassing realization that the reason he was there wasn't a personal interest in me ebbed away, it was replaced by curiosity. He continued, "Physical and mental. Running. Lifting weights. Obstacle courses. Self-defense. Gun safety and sharp shooting."

"Wait." I held a hand up. "What job are you hiring for?"

"I really can't say until you qualify for it. Each assignment is different and confidential. I assure you, though, that you'd be allowed to decline any you're not comfortable with."

Mrs. Allen looked from Everette to her husband. "You're okay with this?"

"We'll talk later," he answered after nodding.

Had Everette shown him a badge? "Are you FBI or something?"

"Nothing so high-class," Everette said.

"So, a private investigator?"

"Something like that. People hire me when they need someone found."

"And you think I'd be good at that?"

"You've already helped locate one young woman. She's safely back home with her parents."

"All I did was overhear a conversation."

"That's half of what I do—listen. Without the information you gave us, we might still be looking for her."

It didn't feel like I'd done anything at all, but I was curious. "And the man with her?"

"There are things I don't ask because I don't need to know. My role was to locate, retrieve, and return."

"You said *we* earlier. Who do you work with?"

"I'm not at liberty to discuss the specifics of what I do unless you end up taking the position and qualifying for a job."

I folded my arms across my chest. "You just saved a young woman who was naïve enough to go off with someone who made vague promises of employment to her. Why would I be stupid enough to do the same?"

"No need to go anywhere. We could start your training right here."

"For a position that doesn't pay much and requires that I learn self-defense as well as gun safety? That doesn't sound like a safe job."

His wide shoulders rose and fell. Before he answered he exchanged a look with Mr. Allen. "It becomes what you make of it. But if you're looking for a way to wake up every day, knowing you're making a difference while getting healthy and learning some new skills, this is your chance."

It was tempting to say yes. Working out had once been something I enjoyed. I hated being afraid all the time. It didn't hurt that being with Everette had me feeling more alive than I had in a long time. "Why me?"

"Why *not* you?"

Why couldn't I track down and save people? Oh, maybe because I'd seen the ugly side of humanity and was still sleeping with a baseball bat next to my bed. "I'm sorry. I'm not interested. Thank you for the offer, though."

My refusal didn't appear unexpected to him. "I suppose I'll just use my time here as a vacation then. Mr. Allen has kindly offered me a room."

What? My gaze flew to Mrs. Allen's face. My unspoken discomfort with that idea was heard and acknowledged.

She nodded toward her husband. "Are you sure that's a good idea, Drew?"

Mr. Allen pinned Everette with a look. "Yes. For now. Everette's here with the best of intentions." His expression turned amused. "Plus, his parents invited us for a visit. They don't seem to have anything to hide. They said we could stay in his room as long as we don't touch his Hulk figurine collection."

He lived with his parents? It was difficult to imagine the man before me as anything but successful and out on his own.

"It's not how it sounds." Everette groaned and blushed. "It's an inside joke. My friends buy me one every year for my birthday and I don't want to just throw them away."

His embarrassment was confusing. On one hand he was physically enormous and bold, but there were glimpses of a softer side to him. Which was he?

Mr. Allen asked, "Well, looks like we have a full house again, Sandy. Do you want help making lunch?"

"Sure," she answered cheerfully. "Everette, would you mind if I speak to your parents as well?"

Holding my gaze, he straightened and stepped back. "No problem. I'll give you their number."

As she and Mr. Allen walked away, her voice carried back to us. "Drew, come to bed early tonight and let's see what we can train each other to do."

He chuckled. "I like the way you think."

Neither Everette nor I said anything for a moment. Eventually, I laughed nervously. "I bet she gave him a run for his money when they dated."

"I'm sure that's something he's never complained about," Everette said so seriously that my eyes flew to his.

He'd said he'd come to offer me a job—a job I'd refused. So, why was he staying?

Chapter Eight

Everette

STANDING SO CLOSE to Shelby was making it difficult for me to think of anything past kissing her again. In Driverton and during my drive back to Rhode Island, I'd told myself that helping her was the only reason she'd been impossible to keep from my thoughts.

Dammit, I hate when Ollie and Levi are right.

No, I wasn't imagining forever with her, but standing there, looking down into her eyes, I felt bonded to her in a way I couldn't remember feeling for another woman. The temptation to lean closer to breathe her in was heady. Levi had teased me about wanting to rescue her and I couldn't deny that I did, but this was more. Perhaps because the details Bradford had given me regarding what had happened to her parents had gutted me. Knowing that pain I'd sensed in her eyes was justified had affected me. I'd always been protective of my family and friends. After my father had been injured at work, I'd given up my dream of joining the military and seeing the world. When my mother had been unable to afford the house on her income as the local seamstress, I'd stepped up to cover their mortgage. And my siblings? I wanted them to have the opportunities I'd lost when my father had been hurt. That's what families did.

Shelby wasn't family, but I wanted to build a wall around her, give her a place she'd always be safe, and promise her that no one would ever hurt her again. It wasn't something I could logically defend. My feelings toward Shelby were primal and territorial. She mattered to me. It was as simple and as confusing as that.

Thankfully I hadn't shared all of that with my friends. They'd still be laughing if I had. Instead, I'd claimed my motivation was solely about helping Shelby through a rough time. It was enough to sway them to also care about Shelby. When Bradford shared what he knew about her life before her parents' deaths, it had been difficult to believe the nervous woman I'd met had once run marathons and had done substantial traveling on her own. She'd been living life boldly and been winning at it. A quick social media scan produced countless photos of her smiling into the camera with confidence and joy in her eyes. Where was that woman now?

Lost.

Not unlike the people Bradford and Cooper had trained me to locate. After much debate on how I'd do it, Ollie, Levi, Bradford, and I decided on a genius plan to help Shelby regain her confidence.

It didn't involve kissing her.

Dating her.

Making her mine.

just above the knee? If you strike a person there it can cause their leg to go numb and can drop someone to the ground. People tend to strike for the crotch, but that's an anticipated move. There's also something called the Georgia Stomp that I could teach you. It's really just throwing all of your weight into one downward stomp on the top of someone's foot. You can take down someone even my size with that move."

She inhaled sharply and her chin rose. "I'd go for the eyes."

Good, at least she had a plan. We could start there. "That works too. The key is to strike first, strike hard, then run. Don't give someone time to prepare or recover. The element of surprise is a powerful tool and putting distance between yourself and a problem can be what saves your life."

"So I shouldn't have given away my signature move." She searched my face. "I can't imagine you running away from anything."

"I get hired to locate, retrieve, and return. How can I do that if I'm dead?" Slowly, I opened the truck and pulled out two pieces of luggage, one much larger than the other. A quick glance down the walkway confirmed that Mr. Allen was watching us from a distance. I liked him more for it. "It's not about giving up. Sometimes you need to fall back, regroup, and find a better way."

"I don't understand you. You're all about safety, but you're okay with having strangers, albeit the Allens, stay with your parents?"

"What could happen? It's a small town." She inhaled audibly and all warmth left her eyes. *Her parents. Shit.* I cursed myself for being thoughtless. "What I mean is I'm from a small town where everyone knows everyone's business and they watch out for each other. Not that bad things only happen in cities, but—" I stopped because I wasn't making things better.

Her eyes narrowed. "You know about my parents." It wasn't a question.

"Yes."

"Is that the reason you offered me a job? You feel bad for me?"

I've never been good at subterfuge. "And if it is?"

I regretted those words as soon as I voiced them. She shook her head and took a step back. "I don't need to be rescued. You can take your luggage, your pity, and your top-secret job and shove them up your—"

"Hey, there," I said in the calming voice I used with my mom's Chihuahua when it retreated to hide under the porch. "You might want to wait until you know me better before you lump me in with those who've done you wrong. There's a high probability I'll mess something up, but give me a little time to earn that anger."

"I can't do this." Her nose reddened as her temper rose. I was tempted to pull her to me for the hug I had a feeling she needed. "You need to leave."

"Because I know what happened to you? Or because I kissed you?"

Her hands fisted at her sides. "Is this some kind of joke to you? Did you see my story online and decide to mess with me?"

Oh, I didn't like the implication that someone had already done that to her. "Do people do that?"

"Sometimes." The wary look returned. "They blame my parents for the fire and the death of the man who broke into their house. I get harassed now and then by strangers who think I'm not sympathetic enough to all the lives lost that day."

"What the fuck is wrong with people?"

Her gaze lowered. "I don't claim the ability to understand anyone anymore."

"No wonder you're angry."

She blinked a few times quickly. "I'm not angry. I'm focusing on being grateful for what I still have."

"Grateful is good." My parents were big believers of the power of gratitude, but Bradford had recently taught me how to channel my anger with myself into positive actions. "Anger can be healthy as well if you redirect it into something positive."

"I'm positive none of this is any of your business and there is no way you and I are staying in the same house. How is that for channeling it?"

"It's the kiss, isn't it? Don't worry about that happening again. It was impulsive. You'd just given me information I knew would help us find that young girl. If it makes you feel better, I can promise you it won't happen again—unless you locate another runaway, then all bets are off because apparently I find that shit exciting."

She did not look amused. Most people liked me, but I was missing the mark when it came to winning Shelby over.

The glare she shot me would have had a lesser man turning tail and giving up. I, however, was riding the high of my short, but perfect, record of saving lives. Winning her over didn't involve dodging bullets. All that was necessary was patience and perseverance. "I don't want you here," she muttered.

I shrugged. "I'm staying anyway."

She made a frustrated sound that I took as progress. "Then I'll leave."

"No, you won't. You like it here."

She inhaled sharply, then shook her head. "You know what? I don't care. Stay. Go. It doesn't matter to me."

She had every reason to not trust strangers, but that's what made this a worthwhile quest. One day, she'd thank me for not giving up on her. I could see her, back at Little Willie's, telling everyone I was the reason she was doing better. I'd deny being responsible and claim it was all her and my only role had been to nudge her toward happiness again . . .

"Why are you smiling?" she demanded, her hands going to her hips.

I hadn't realized I was. "Sorry. I was thinking about how great it'll be when you change your mind about training with me."

"Not going to happen."

I placed the largest piece of luggage in front of her. "Think you can take this one or is it too heavy for you?"

"Did you not just hear me say I don't want you here?"

"What are you afraid of?" I nodded toward the path. "If

it's me, Mr. Allen is supervising this exchange so you're safe."

When her eyes met mine again, her bottom lip quivered. "I do feel safe here. Please don't take that from me." Whoosh. I handed her a corner of my heart right there and then.

"I would never hurt you. I'm here to help you."

I'd expected an entirely different response than the one she gave me. "I. Don't. Need. You. You think you're the first man to want to save me? You should call Jeff so you can hear how badly that worked out for him."

I didn't love the name of another man on her lips, but I had to ask. "Who's Jeff?"

For a moment she didn't appear willing to tell me, but then fire flashed in her eyes. "Maybe the truth will get you to go. I moved in with him after—after. He felt bad for me too. He was a really nice guy. And what did that get him? Nothing, because I have nothing to give anyone." Her laugh was nervous and wild. "I am not in a good place mentally. I've got nothing going for me and nothing to lose. Full disclosure, I'm hanging on to my sanity by a thread so I wouldn't fuck around with me. I'm not right."

It was a lot to absorb. She really wasn't doing well. "So . . . the smaller luggage?" I asked as I placed my second bag beside the first.

Her mouth opened and closed before she reached for the larger bag. "I'm not weak."

"I never said you were."

She turned and began to roll the luggage up the path. I quickly closed the trunk, grabbed the smaller bag and followed her. Halfway up the path, she spun around and waved a finger up at me. "Don't tell Mrs. Allen about what I said about not having anything to lose. She's been encouraging me to write down the things I'm grateful for and I don't want her to think she's wasting her time with me. It's helping . . ."

I nodded. What a curious woman she was. She kept telling me she had nothing to give anyone, but even when cornered she worried about the feelings of others. I had no doubt that I was meant to help her. "Tell me what you need. Talk to me."

"You don't even know me."

"Being here will change that."

"Why are you trying so hard?" Her eyes narrowed. "If you're hoping we'll hook up, I'm essentially asexual now."

"Challenge accepted." I bit back a smile. "But first let's see if we can get you physically fit."

Her mouth dropped open. "What did you just say?"

Had that come out wrong? For someone who seemed timid around men she looked ready to castrate me. "Exercise releases endorphins which helps a person feel better. My moods have improved since I started running every day. Sex between us is off the table until you're feeling better about yourself."

"Buddy, there is zero chance of you and me having sex."

"Today." I shot her a playful smile. "Who knows how you'll feel after you start muscling up."

Shaking her head, that sad look darkened her eyes again. "I don't get you. None of this is funny to me."

I sighed and remembered the many times Mrs. Williams had accused Levi, Ollie, and me of not being serious enough. The more uncomfortable a situation was, the more jokes we made. That wasn't what she needed, though. In a quiet tone, I said, "I told you I'd come back for you and here I am."

"But why?"

It was a valid question. Obviously I was attracted to her, but she didn't want to hear that. "Someone came into my life recently and changed it for the better. I'm here to pay that forward."

"Because you met me briefly and decided I'm qualified for whatever it is you do?"

I took her questions as a good sign. It was an improvement from snarling that she wanted me to leave. "I was struggling until I met someone who offered me what I'm offering you. I understand your doubts. I had the same. But I gave it a chance. First, he got me moving, then gave me a lot to think about, and finally taught me skills I could use not to just defend myself but to also save others. I was afraid my life was passing me by. Now I feel empowered—capable of almost anything."

"That sounds nice, actually." The battle that raged within her shone in her eyes. "I remember feeling that way. This wasn't always me."

"So, train with me. What do you have to lose?"

"I do need to do something." Her shoulders rose and fell. "I don't go anywhere without Mace. I can't sleep without a baseball bat beside my bed and even then, I frequently wake up afraid I'll find someone in my house. I hate that I can't go back to who I used to be. I miss my parents, my old friends—but mostly *me*. I'm doing my best to focus on being grateful, but I remember what it was like to not fear the shadows." Pain twisted her otherwise beautiful lips. "You think your training could fix that?"

"Yes." I wouldn't have been there if I didn't believe that. "It won't make it all go away, but it'll give you the strength to better deal with it."

Her hands clenched the handle of the luggage. "One day. I'll give you one day and if I'm not comfortable with any part of what you ask me to do, we're done."

"Yes," I said and closed the distance between us in a rush. "You won't regret it." She was so damn beautiful. I bent until my lips hovered above hers, then caught myself just in time. "Sorry about that. I was so excited you agreed I almost kissed you again. I'll get control of that."

She gave me an odd look, then turned and started up the path again, rolling my luggage beside her. It was probably wrong of me to take the opportunity to appreciate her perfectly rounded ass, but I'm only human.

And she'd said yes.

Chapter Nine

Shelby

LATER THAT NIGHT I tossed and turned rather than sleeping. Only a thin wall divided me from the man who had me so confused I'd spent most of the day hiding in my room. If I put aside the fact that he was drop-dead gorgeous and could likely have any woman he set his eyes on, his interest in me still made no sense.

I wasn't model material, but I wasn't butt ugly either. Outwardly I didn't look like the mess I was on the inside. Sure, I wasn't as toned as I'd once been, but I was healthy-ish. My stomach had some roundness to it and my sides were thicker, but it was nothing I couldn't tuck into jeans after I'd sized up. It wasn't inconceivable that someone could be attracted to me. Jeff had been.

However, I'd outright told him I was a basket case. When a woman looks a man in the eye and tells him she's not right—how was that not the biggest turnoff?

I was beginning to wonder if Megan had sent him. Not in the kind of mystical way Mrs. Allen considered possible. There was a slim chance Megan had hired someone to watch over me. It was a stretch, and neither of us had the cash for something like that, but how else could Everette's determination to stay and train me be explained?

I tossed over onto my other side and hugged a pillow to me. Lunch with Everette and the Allens had only left me with more questions. Mrs. Allen kept looking back and forth between Everette and me with a smile as if waiting for us to announce that we were a couple. It made me wonder what the heck Mr. Allen had told her.

All through the meal I watched for some sign that Everette couldn't be trusted. He was friendly without being overly so. None of Mr. Allen's questions seemed to make him uncomfortable. If he was hiding something, he'd perfected looking calm about it.

If everything Everette said was to be believed, he'd spent his entire life in a small town. The oldest of three children, Everette was indeed still living with his parents. His father had been seriously injured on the job when Everette was in high school. When his mother had struggled to make enough to keep the house, Everette had taken over the household bills.

As if it were the most normal thing for a man in his midtwenties, Everette said, "I'm broke most of the time, but I am putting both of my younger siblings through college so I hear that's normal."

"You're paying for college for your siblings?" No. I had to have heard that wrong.

His smile was modest when he said, "They both have scholarships as well, but yes. Someone had to. They deserve a chance for more than life in a small town if that's what they want. I couldn't do it, though, without the support of my community. There were times when I came up short and my friends held a fundraiser to help out. That's a common occurrence where I come from. We don't have much, but we have each other."

I'd had to look away to hide the longing his words filled me with. I didn't have a home anymore or a community. I'd grown up in a good area, but not one where the neighbors did more than wave to each other. Was that why they didn't seem bothered when my parents' lawn had become a shrine to someone who'd never lived there?

What would it be like to live in a town where people watched out for each other? The more Everette described the town he'd grown up in, the more I understood why he felt his parents were safe there. It was a town outside of time, diverse but closely bonded, and so damn perfect I wasn't sure he hadn't made it up as part of another alias.

No one asked me about my town or my family, which was actually a relief. I didn't want to be a downer, but short of lying, there wasn't much good I could say about my current situation that wouldn't have been in stark contrast to the utopia Everette lived in.

After lunch, Everette asked me if I was okay starting the next day with a morning run. I said I was even though I was conflicted about whether or not I wanted to be alone with him again. In front of the Allens he'd acted like he and I were simply two guests having idle conversation with our hosts.

Had he not announced on the walk back from his car that he'd almost kissed me again, I wouldn't have thought he was attracted to me.

If he even is.

Not that I want him to be.

Rolling over again, I threw an arm over my eyes and kicked off the blanket in irritation. I'd found a place that might actually be healthy for me. All my energy should have been focused on getting a job and filling that gratitude journal with happy thoughts.

I'd just left a man behind because men weren't the solution.

I needed to find my own strength.

Maybe going for a run will help clear my head. I used to love to start my day with one before ... just before. I didn't need to worry if I had my running shoes with me. Sadly, everything I owned was in my room or stuffed in my car.

I groaned as I remembered how pathetic I'd sounded when I told Everette I'd found a place I felt safe and begged him not to take that away from me. If there was a chance exercise would help me get past sounding like a scared orphan left on a corner, I had to give it a try.

One thought led to another until memories from the past began to weave in and out of everything else I was worried about. I knew I wouldn't sleep, so I sat up, turned on the light beside my bed, and reached for my gratitude journal.

After dating it, I wrote:

Today I'm grateful for Mr. and Mrs. Allen—for

their support and their protection.

For Megan for finding this place for me.

For a working computer that allowed me to apply for jobs I hope are hiring.

For being strong enough to not completely embarrass myself when I chose to carry Everette's heavy bag into the house.

As a joke I added: **And for hot men with bulging biceps.**

I smiled at that last sentence because it was the toast I'd made with Mrs. Allen. Trusting Everette was definitely a struggle, but if I was honest with myself I would have been disappointed if he'd left when I'd told him to.

It was tempting to call Megan and tell her about Everette, but I didn't want her to think I was about to rush into another relationship just because a man said all the right things to me. I wanted to move forward, not backward.

A glance at the time on my phone confirmed that it was well past midnight. *I'm going to be exhausted tomorrow.*

I should probably cancel.

Damn, I don't have his number.

Well, I suppose he'll figure it out when I don't show up at breakfast.

Chapter Ten

Everette

BOOT CAMP WASN'T about sleeping in or tiptoeing around people's feelings. Bradford had hauled me out of bed the first day at four in the morning. I waited until six before I knocked on Shelby's door. When she didn't answer, I knocked again—louder.

"Go away," she grumbled.

"I'm not going anywhere so you might as well get up, get dressed, and get out here." I did my best to sound as badass as Bradford had.

There was the sound of feet padding toward the door. When it flew open, I was greeted by a tousled, still flushed from sleep, grumpy beauty. She was dressed in flowered cotton shorts and a thin matching top that did a wonderfully poor job of concealing her nipples. I tried not to notice how they hardened as she looked me over. If she was attracted to me, I didn't want to know—not yet. I needed to focus like someone's life depended on it, because I had the feeling hers might. "Get dressed, Princess. The sun is up and that means your first training day has begun."

"I didn't sleep well."

I could tell, but I had a hunch that was nothing new. Moving would help her with that. "I don't care what you run in, you're not backing out before the day has even started. I'll carry your ass to the street if I have to."

She folded her arms beneath those beautiful breasts of hers. "I'd like to see you try."

I coughed in surprise. Her hair was practically standing on end which, when paired with her bad attitude, was so fucking hot. Scaring her was the last thing I wanted to do, but she didn't look afraid of me—she was as turned on by the idea of me hauling her out of there as I was becoming.

Damn.

Adulting was hard. I'd been raised to treat every woman the way I'd want someone to treat my sister. The problem was—Shelby had my body going haywire and my thoughts filling with ideas that had nothing to do with respecting her and everything to do with replacing our planned run with a romp on the bed I could see behind her. I fought to keep my gaze above her shoulders. Leaning in a little, I growled, "Would you?"

Her eyes widened, but not with fear. Breathing became nearly impossible as I waited for her reaction. "You wouldn't do it."

The old me might not have, but the new me had a little cockiness to him. "Be real sure of that before you try me."

She swallowed visibly and seemed to be determining if I was serious.

Giving her another verbal nudge, I said, "The more time

you waste, the longer we'll run."

She looked about to say something, then yawned and stretched. "I actually enjoy running." The move pulled that thin material tight over her nipples. I nearly melted into a pool of my own drool. Was running with an erection uncomfortable? I was about to find out.

"Then get your ass dressed for it." My attempt to sound commanding was undermined by how fucking turned on I was.

She nodded. "Okay. Sorry. I really didn't sleep well and that puts me in a bad mood."

I glanced at my watch. "Oh, look at that, we're fresh out of time for excuses."

"Okay. Okay. Give me five."

"You have two. I'll wait here."

She closed the door in my face, but returned in a heart-beat, dressed, sadly, much more appropriately. Her hair was tied back in a ponytail, and other than the dark circles under her eyes, she looked amazing. "Ready."

We had made it down the stairs and were heading to-ward the door, when Mrs. Allen stopped us. "Going for a walk?" she asked.

"A run," I answered. "I thought we'd head over to the playground. I scoped it out last night and it has work-out stations."

"Well, have fun. I can move breakfast to whenever you're ready for it. Don't rush. Take a shower when you get back." She winked at Shelby. "Separately. Together. This is a no-judgment house."

Shelby tripped over a corner of the rug. I caught her, hauling her to me, then realized she was pressed against the hard evidence of how attracted I was to her, and hastily set her back from me. Our eyes met for one brief, heated second before we both looked away. Her voice was breathless when she said, "Bye and thank you," then bolted out the door.

Mrs. Allen waved for me to wait. "I called your mother last night. She thought Drew and I were sculpture clients of yours. I don't like lies."

"I don't either." I grimaced. "I do sell sculptures. Searching for runaways was an opportunity that came recently. I'll tell my parents about what I'm doing eventually, but for now it's better if they don't know the details. The people I work with are brought in to find those the normal system can't. To succeed, they play outside the law. It can be dangerous both physically and legally. The less my parents or anyone around me knows, the safer they'll be."

The look she gave me was similar to one my mother gave me each time she heard I was heading anywhere with Levi and Ollie. Finally, Mrs. Allen smiled and waved for me to go. "I believe you. Drew told me you came here with a plan for how to help Shelby."

"Yes, ma'am."

"A person would have to be blind to not see that you're also attracted to her."

"That's a distraction I'm putting on the back burner for now. I really think I can help her."

"I like you, Everette. I hope you succeed—on both fronts."

There was such a sparkle in her eyes, I couldn't resist saying, "If you were thirty years younger, Mrs. Allen, I'd be torn between two incredible women."

She laughed again, but looked pleased. "If Drew was thirty years younger, he'd kick your ass for even joking about that."

I nodded. "I get it. It's like that when you find someone special."

"Yes, it is. Now, go. She's waiting for you."

The sight of Shelby bent over and stretching temporarily destroyed my ability to think or move. I froze at the top of the porch steps and took in the perfection of her. Her legs were long and lean. The shorts she'd chosen went from modest to decadent as she moved from one stretch pose to another. When she saw me, she straightened and shot me a shy smile. "Sorry about before. I'm awake now and ready."

Sorry? I couldn't think of a single thing she'd done wrong. Shaking my head, I started down the steps and choked out, "Good, then let's go."

I could have started slowly, but I wanted to clear my head so I sprinted past her and down the path I'd explored the night before. Would she follow me? Could she keep up? I didn't slow down. She needed to want this.

She appeared at my side, smiled, then passed me. The view was impressive and informative. Her pace was quick and even with very little bounce. She kept her head up, her shoulders square and her arms swinging back and forth with a relaxed, but powerful cadence. Oh, yes, I could imagine her running marathons.

When she slowed her speed, I matched it. "You look good," I said. Then groaned inwardly, and added, "As a runner. You look like this isn't new to you."

"Like I said, I enjoy it. I used to run marathons."

"And you will again."

She shot me quite the side-eye, but kept running. "Sorry I made you come to my room this morning. I should have met you downstairs, ready to go."

Memories of how she'd looked in her doorway sent my already thudding heart beating faster. "I didn't mind. We all have days like that. Who knows, tomorrow you might have to drag me out of my bed—" I stopped there as I imagined the possibilities that would spring from that scenario.

She didn't touch that one. The two of us continued on in a comfortable, matched pace. Eventually, she asked, "How much of what you said to the Allens last night was true?"

Her question took me by surprise until I remembered I'd been using a different name when we'd first met. It made sense that it would take time for her to trust me. "All of it."

"Your town is really that wonderful?"

I shrugged. "Every coin has two sides. When you grow up in a place where everyone knows your name, they also know everything else about you. The good. The bad. And it can be difficult to change when everyone sees you a certain way."

"What did you want to change?"

The first thing that came to my mind was a joke, but that was a pattern I was consciously working to break. There was definitely room in my life for humor, but I'd used it as a shield in the past and I didn't need that crutch anymore. And talking about my feelings? That was new to me as well. "How much do you want to know?"

She also took a moment before responding. "As much as you're comfortable sharing, I guess."

"My comfort level when it comes to talking about how I feel on most subjects is zero, but I also want you to know me, so ask away."

We both said nothing as we made our way up and down a small hill, then she said, "I used to be comfortable talking about myself and my feelings. When I fell apart, there was less and less of me I shared. I wanted to be strong for the people who loved me. And I was afraid to be weak in front of those who didn't. I kind of kept everything to myself, but this is good. I want to get to know you. And I feel like I can show you the real me."

I nearly tripped over nothing as I remembered how much she'd shown me that morning.

Focus. That's not what she was referring to. I slowed my pace a bit more because I didn't want to break our connection and I hadn't run marathons. "You can."

"What did you want to change about yourself?"

"In the beginning—everything. I was like a fallen tree in the forest. There was nothing immediately appealing or promising about me, or so I thought. But I was reminded by a friend that the quality of the core matters more than outward appearances. I began to see that I was more than my bad habits. I had value and potential."

She gave me another side look. "You didn't know that?"

In response to the intensity of her gaze, I said, "I've always been a good son, brother, and friend. And according to some women from the surrounding town, a good fuck as well. I wanted to be more than that."

Shelby laughed then choked and gasped for air. "Sorry I was not expecting that last part."

"That I'd be good in bed?" I was a little offended. "Don't worry I'll bring it when we get to that point."

"*When?*" she asked with a half laugh. "That's bold, don't you think? I already told you that's not an option."

"Are we being real with each other or not?"

"Did you not hear what I told you about Jeff? I literally lived with him for four months and nothing happened. I don't want to lead you on, but I'm not in a place where—"

I moved in front of her and stopped abruptly, lifting her off her feet as her momentum brought her up against me. Our bodies slammed into each other, but I raised her easily until her face was level with mine. Shock widened her eyes, but she didn't struggle. "Did Jeff ever pick you up, strip you down, throw your legs over his shoulders and feast on you until you came so much you couldn't remember your name?"

Her voice was a husky squeak. "No."

Holding her gaze, and control over my desire, I ground out, "Then Jeff and I are not the same man." We were both shining with sweat and breathing heavily. It would have been easy to give in to the pull of her, but confidence gave me patience. This wasn't just about me and what I wanted. I lowered her to her feet and took a step back. "But there's no rush for that. First, you train."

All eyes, and looking a little dazed, she asked, "For the job?"

I smiled at that. "Is there a second option?"

"No," she said once, then more emphatically. "Of course not."

She was so damn serious, I probably shouldn't have, but I joked, "I don't know if I'm into any other kind of training, but for you, I'd at least read up on it."

"I said no to anything more." Her voice was breathless and sending an entirely different message than her words.

I rolled a hand through the air. "It was a little ambiguous. Guys are eternally hopeful. Be direct. I'll give you an example. Touch my arm."

"Why?"

"To show you how to be clear enough for any man."

She gave me a long look then laid her hand on my arm. I shrugged her touch off and said, "Don't fucking touch me."

She smiled. "That *is* clear."

"And it should always be respected. I'll teach you how to handle it if it ever isn't." I brought my hands back to her waist and lifted her so we were eye to eye again. "For now, let's say I did something like this and you wanted to be clear about how you felt about it, what would you say?"

"I—I'd—I—" Her face went pink and *yes* battled with *no* in her eyes.

Slowly I lowered her back to her feet. "See, that's why nothing can happen between us yet. I'd wait even if you asked . . . although *maybe* if you begged . . . no I'd like to think I'd hold to my decision to help you first—"

"Everette."

"Yes?"

"Where is this playground we're going to?"

"About a mile more down this path."

"I'll race you there."

Without giving me time to agree, she took off in a sprint. Now, I've often heard it said that men enjoy a good chase, but I had no idea how literally that could be taken. She was impressively fast, and I was all in.

Chapter Eleven

Shelby

*O*H, MY GOD.
  I'm not asexual at all.
Holy shit.
And he is nothing like Jeff.

I ran as fast as I ever had. The adrenaline coursing through me wasn't from fear—at least not of him. He had me feeling alive and full of anticipation. I had no idea how to handle that. It had been months since I'd felt anything. Any motivation I'd summoned to move forward had been forced. I hadn't felt excited about anything since . . .

The realization that I wanted to do anything with Everette was terrifying. It was too much, too fast. That meant it wasn't real, didn't it?

With Everette, there would be no running away and hiding. He'd never allow that. He had plans for me—some seemingly pure in nature and some very much not. With him, I felt vulnerable and exposed, but also wildly hopeful.

When he'd picked me up as if I weighed nothing, I'd wanted to melt into his strength. Jeff had been another person in the bed at night, which should have made me feel secure, but hadn't. Everette had a confidence and presence that had me feeling both vulnerable and safe at the same time.

What did I do with a man like that? I kept running away from him. That's what I did. A quick glance back confirmed that so far it had done nothing to deter him. He was a few feet back—gaining on me. A hunter closing in on his prey. Was the chase as exciting for him as it was for me?

I came to an air-gasping stop when the trail opened to a small field. There was a large playground on one side and a mulched area with workout stations on the other. He stopped beside me. Side by side, we bent over to catch our breath. I said, "I didn't realize how quickly I could get out of shape."

"I was thinking that same thing."

He was joking, and I almost laughed, but my body was warming beneath his attention the way it did every time he looked at me. Attempting to lessen the sexual tension, I straightened and said, "And yet faster than you."

Still bent over, he smiled up at me. "Or I was enjoying the view too much to take the lead." The wink he shot me temporarily robbed me of my ability to speak. It was impossible to tear my gaze away as he unfolded to his full height.

How could he ever have thought there was nothing appealing about him? All I saw when I looked at him was a confident, gorgeous man in his prime. There was something I had to know. "What kind of bad habits?"

"Sorry?"

"You said you realized you were more than your bad habits. What was it that you were doing?"

He nodded his head toward the workout area and we started to make our way toward it. "There wasn't a lot to do in the town I grew up in. We all partied hard in high school. A lot of people I knew left after they graduated. Some came back. Some didn't. For those of us who stayed behind, the party didn't end."

There was a humility to him when he spoke that had me wanting to comfort him. "You stayed to help your parents. That's beautiful."

"Necessary yes. Beautiful? Not really." As soon as he reached a set of three low bars, he began to do push-ups off the one that was a couple of feet high. When he finished, he moved on to the next. "Do twenty on each."

My upper body strength had never been impressive, but I didn't refuse. If my form wasn't correct, he didn't mention it. When he dropped down to the lowest bar, I moved over to the one he'd finished with and said, "This job you're training me for, is that how you support your family?"

"No. Finding runaways doesn't pay well. Some families do pay for the services, but most of that money goes toward a fund to help families who can't afford us."

I did five slow push-ups. Stopped, then did five more. I was about to stand and announce that was all I could do, when his eyes met mine and he commanded, "Ten more."

"My arms are shaking."

There was steel in his gaze that was hot as hell. "Do it."

No was on the tip of my tongue. I'd always been an independent woman who didn't take orders from a man. I didn't owe this one anything. Still, I didn't want to refuse him . . . so I did five more. The last one almost didn't happen and I had to lock my arms at the elbow to hold myself up.

My body went into sensory overload when he crouched and reached beneath me. His fingers splayed across my lower rib cage. His thumb came to rest just below my breasts. "You've got this," he said softly. "One at a time."

Could I do that without breathing? I tore my gaze from his and lowered myself toward the bar again. With his support, I didn't collapse as I'd feared I might. Rising was easier as well. After completing one more, I paused. Lord, his touch was heavenly. Steady. Strong. I pumped out three more push-ups then froze.

Did he expect me to do twenty more on the lowest bar as he had? Without looking at him, I said, "I've never been good at push-ups."

"You will be," he said easily. When he removed his hand, I felt none of the relief I would have expected—only disappointment. "One bar left. Do you want my help?"

I stood and moved to stand in front of the last bar. His question was about the task before me, but as I looked up into his eyes it felt like agreeing to this was agreeing to everything he had planned for me.

Could I do this? Could I actually become not only not afraid, but also confident like him? Did I see myself tracking down runaways and helping them return home?

And us—were we even possible?

Was I willing to risk caring about someone again? I'd told myself I had what it took to go on alone. Would saying yes to him leave me feeling better or so much worse?

"Talk to me, Shelby."

I inhaled a shaky breath. "I don't know if I can do this."

He leaned down until we were eye to eye. "I do. You're stronger than you know. Trust me and I'll prove it to you."

"I don't want to need your help."

His hand came up to wipe a bead of sweat from my temple. "Suck it up, Buttercup, you're stuck with me for now. Stop focusing on who you are today and start thinking about how good it'll feel to tell me you don't need me anymore and mean it."

Is that where we were headed? Of course it was. He'd offered me a chance to work with him. He was anticipating a day when the two of us would have sex. Neither of those two things required he had feelings for me. "Five more," I offered.

"Twenty."

"Ten."

"Twenty-five."

"That's not how negotiating works."

"I'm not negotiating with you. Thirty. Now get down on your knees."

My eyes widened and my sex took what he'd said entirely the wrong way. My body hummed with a hunger I'd thought was no longer possible. My tongue flicked across my lower lip. Maybe it was time to say yes instead of no.

Confirmation that he was not a mind reader came when

he added, "It's a modification you can use to make it easier."

"For the push-ups," I reminded myself and turned away from him. I sank to my knees, but then rose onto my toes and waited. "I'd rather do it this way." Just as I'd thought, his hand slid beneath me again. I gasped from the pleasure of that touch.

"Good girl," he said in a tone I imagined him using if I held off an orgasm until he told me I could come. "This time keep going. Don't stop. I've got you."

Yes, you do.

There was still effort required on my part. He didn't lift me. But when we reached thirty, I was so turned on I would gladly have done several more sets.

"You did it." His smile when I finished was so genuine I felt a little guilty about how many times I'd imagined him naked and beneath me. He stood and held out that amazing hand of his. I scrambled to my feet without taking it. "Didn't it feel good to finish?"

Was he speaking in innuendoes or was I thinking in them? The way his eyes darkened when he looked at me and his cheeks flushed hinted that it could be a combination of both. "It did," I said with a sigh and a husky chuckle.

"Next we'll do the vertical cargo net. We'll time each other."

"Oh," I said breathlessly, "I didn't realize faster was better."

Without missing a beat, he said, "It is when you need to get over a fence and someone is chasing you."

Okay. So, we're not actually talking about sex.

Of course, we're not.

"Right. That makes sense. You go first. I'll watch you." See, that sounds raunchy too. What is wrong with me? "I mean, I'll time you."

"Then I'll watch you."

Wait. *Is* he flirting with me?

We walked over to the cargo net wall that rose higher than I would have expected for a playground to want, but the space did seem made for dual purposes. He handed me his phone with a timer on the screen. "Don't be discouraged if your first time isn't your best. Everything gets better with practice." His lips twisted in a smirk.

He's definitely flirting. With the best blank expression I could muster, I asked, "Even you?"

Delight lit his eyes. "I'd like to think I'm good right out the gate, but there's a learning curve with everyone."

Humble and bold. Interesting and dangerously likeable. I hit the start button for the timer and waved the screen at him. "Go."

He spun and sprinted the short distance to the net and was up and over it with intimidating speed. Although he had the height and breadth of a linebacker, he was remarkably agile.

And gorgeous.

And walking toward me with a big smile that warmed me to my toes. What would all that athleticism translate to in the bedroom?

"I know what you're thinking—"

"I don't think you do."

"You haven't done this since you were a kid—or maybe ever. You don't want to look stupid in front of me. But don't worry. I'm here to cheer you on, not judge you."

"It's like you can read my mind," I lied weakly. I was more concerned with whatever this sizzle was between us than my ability to climb a playground net, but I wasn't about to admit that.

"The only person who would judge someone for ungracefully hauling themselves over that wall, is someone who probably couldn't get their own ass over it. I've stood where you are, tried to climb it, fallen, and gotten back up. The only way you can fail is if you give up. So, forget I'm here and just do it."

"Forget you're here." Yeah, that wasn't possible.

"We don't have to time you today. Your first time shouldn't be stressful."

I opened my mouth to accuse him of deliberately phrasing it that way, then decided not to embarrass myself just in case he hadn't. "Here's your phone." I handed it to him then strode toward the netting and let my competitive nature take over. I was up and over it in a time that might not have beaten his, but at least would have rivaled it.

And it felt good.

"Damn, okay. You're already good at that."

Smiling, I said, "It's all in the legs. I used to do a lot of legwork for running."

"Gotcha. So it's really your upper body that needs conditioning."

I frowned. "I guess."

He pointed toward the pull-up bar. "Then that's where we're headed next."

I groaned. "I've never been able to do a pull-up."

Heat returned to his gaze. "I'll help you."

I opened my mouth to say that wouldn't be necessary, then snapped it shut without uttering a sound. I imagined him standing so close I could feel the heat of his body. His hands would close on my sides. He'd lift me, then ever so slowly slide me down his muscled front. Did I really want to say no to that? I cleared my throat. "Okay."

A moment later I was hanging from a bar, waiting for my fantasy to become a reality. He was sadly a few feet away and I wasn't prepared for the laugh that rumbled out of him. "You have to at least try."

"This is me trying," I ground out.

He stepped closer and pretended to inspect my biceps. "There's not even a little bit of muscle in there?"

"Fuck you."

He barked out a laugh. "That's the spirit. Get mad and direct some of that energy to your arms."

I tightened my arms and rose up a few inches, then slumped back to where I was. "I told you I wasn't good at this." Why had I thought this would be sexy?

"Come on, I've seen little old ladies able to haul themselves higher than that."

He was really beginning to piss me off. I lifted myself higher and after I lowered myself, tried again. "If you think I'm doing this again after today, you're delusional."

"A little less whining and you just might be able to get

that chin over the bar."

"I thought you were nice."

"And I thought you weren't weak."

That was it. A surge of anger shot through me, and I lifted myself up until my chin cleared the bar. Instantly his hands were on my rib cage, guiding me back down. "See, you can do it."

"You called me weak."

"I did. I knew it would rile you."

In a tone thick with sarcasm, I asked, "Is that part of the training? Pissing me off to motivate me?"

"When necessary, yes."

"It's a surefire way to get me to not like you."

"I'm not worried about that."

"Because you think you're irresistible?"

He chuckled. "You're adorable when you're angry."

I lifted myself up and over the bar with very little help from him. "And you're getting less attractive by the moment."

"Really?" This time when he lowered me, my breasts brushed against his chest and we both sucked in a breath. "Is that so?"

Blood pumping, I pushed off him by arching my body and banged out two impressive chin-ups. "Yes." Sadly my answer came out like a breathy invitation rather than a confirmation of my claim.

"Good, because my goal is to motivate you." A sexy smile pulled at his lips. "So far my methods are working."

Yes, they were. How could I refuse him while hanging

from the bar, supported mostly by his hands on my rib cage? My heart was racing, my body craving more of his touch.

"Five more chin-ups."

I tried and failed. Tried again and failed again. The third time I struggled to lift myself, he supported me. After the second one, I said, "That's all I've got."

"Three more."

"I'm done."

"Four."

"I don't work for or with you yet. You don't actually get to boss me around." I began to remove my hands from the bar in anticipation of him lowering me.

He lifted me a few inches, nuzzled the space between his hands and growled against my skin. "Five. Don't do them for me. Do them for you."

Fire shot through me and it was all I could do to not wrap my legs around him and beg to be taken right there. There was nothing I would have denied him in that moment, not my body, not his demand. With his help, I lifted myself five more times. When I finished he set me on the ground before him. Neither of us spoke at first. He looked as turned on as I was and I wondered if his resolve would crumble if I told him I wanted him.

I didn't test him, though. He was right. I wasn't ready. My body was, but my emotions were still all over the place. In a croak, I asked, "Is this what your training was like?"

He laughed. "Not at all. When you meet Bradford, you'll understand."

"Bradford?"

His expression closed as if he'd said something he hadn't meant to. "Just a friend of mine."

"The friend who trained you for your top-secret missions." It sounded ridiculous when said like that, but Everette didn't smile or deny it.

"You ready for your first self-defense lesson?"

Considering how our workout session had gone, I wasn't sure if I was ready to fend him off, or if I would even want to. "Depends on what it entails."

He nodded. "We'll start simple. When I came up on you that first day, you handled the situation well. Distance is often the best defense and should be your first choice. If it's not an option or if leaving would put you in a less secure location, look around for support. Don't let size determine who you choose to go up to for help. Intention trumps muscle. Mothers. Fathers. Men or women who already seem to be aware that something is going down. These people will usually help."

"I've seen videos where people advise going up to men and pretending you've been looking for them."

"You can do the same with women. I've seen all kinds of people step up. The key is to ask one specific person for help. If you ask a crowd, there's a chance everyone will assume someone else will help you. You pick one person. Look them in the eye. And it's a rare person who can walk away from that. I don't care if you're appealing to someone with a criminal past, in that moment, they're involved, and that's powerful."

"That makes sense."

"Now, let's say you're alone and you don't have your Mace with you. I'm approaching you. What should you do? There's no time to run."

"I'd take a photo of your face because it uploads instantly. So, even if you smash my phone, the police could still find you."

"Honestly, I've never thought of that. If there's time to take a photo, I'd tell the attacker that last part. But let's say you've turned to face me and I rush up and grab you."

I wasn't prepared for the force with which he came at me and swung me over one of his shoulders. I expected fear to follow, but that wasn't at all how my body was interpreting being hauled around by him.

"What are you going to do now?" he asked.

So, so many possibilities were running through my head, but not one of them involved fighting him off. "Um—"

"This is one of the worst-case scenarios because you can't use your weight against me. If the attacker is worried you'll make noise, he might try to punch you in the head or hit your head against something. You'll have to act fast. Wrap your arm around my neck. Cup your fingers under my chin. Bring your other arm around if you can and grab hold of your hand. Gain control of my head. Use every bit of strength in your arms to choke me."

I positioned my hands as he instructed, but didn't tighten them. The last thing I wanted to do was hurt him or anyone.

He gave my ass a not-so-gentle smack. "Listen Princess, I'm not here to waste my time or yours. You want the chance to work with me, prove you deserve it. Or tell me you're weak and scared and I'll put you down."

"I'm not weak."

"Prove it."

"I don't want to hurt you."

"You couldn't if you tried." He gave my ass another slap, just a tad bit harder.

It was enough to irk me. I tightened my arm around his neck and pulled one hand with another. He coughed. I tightened more, he gagged and loosened his arms enough that I was able to position my knee against his chest and use the strongest part of my body to break free of his grasp. I did fall, but I scrambled backward and was on my feet quickly.

"Good girl," he said.

Breathing heavily, I snapped, "First, don't call me a girl. I'm a woman. Second, I've watched videos on self-defense and there was no ass slapping."

His grin was unapologetic. "I was improvising."

"You expect me to believe that?"

"You're right. I'm having a hard time keeping my hands to myself."

"Is that a chronic problem?"

"Only since we met." His smile widened and humor lit his gaze. "My career as a personal self-defense trainer may need to begin and end with you. I knew you'd be trouble."

I doubt there was a woman alive who could have stayed irritated with him if he smiled at her like that. Slowly, I allowed myself to smile back. "Me?"

"Sure. There you were, in need of being helped just

when I was learning how to be a hero. I came back with the purest of intentions, but you won't stop looking at me like you'd like to jump my bones. So, yeah, trouble."

"Oh, my God, I cannot be the only one who wants to smack some of the smugness out of you."

"Hold on, so you *do* like it rough?"

I laughed at that even while I struggled to label what I felt toward him. He could irritate me one second, turn me on the next, then somehow have me laughing through what normally would have been an uncomfortable situation and feeling like we were old friends. "With you—maybe." I'd meant to imply that he could drive me to violence, but that wasn't how he took it.

"Well, okay then." After a moment, he cleared his throat and said, "Are you up for another run?"

"Absolutely."

He took off at a good clip. I caught up to him easily. When I fell into step beside him, he said, "We can do more self-defense training tomorrow."

Promise? I held back the smile that had almost accompanied that thought. "I'll think about it."

Chapter Twelve

Everette

A S WE RAN, I took the opportunity to lecture myself on deviating from my plan. I was there to help her, but she was so damn tempting it was becoming increasingly difficult to remember that I wasn't there to make her mine.

"How far are we going to go today?" she asked.

That was the question my lower half kept asking. "I'm determined not to rush this."

She shot me a quick look. "The run. Are we going all the way around the lake or doubling back at some point?"

Right. "If you're up to it, the whole loop is eight miles with reasonably good footing for most of it."

"Wait, you're giving me a choice?"

I took the humor in her voice as a sign that I was winning her over to the idea of training with me for more than one day. "You can run it or walk it. All you're not allowed to do is quit." That last part filled my thoughts with a quick fantasy of tossing her over my shoulder again. I groaned. Not since high school had it been necessary to imagine someone fifty years older and toothless to be able to speak to a beautiful woman without all of my blood heading south. It worked until I made the mistake of glancing at Shelby. Flushed and sweaty, with her breasts bouncing up and down and her muscled legs pumping, she was breathtaking.

I expected her to protest, but she didn't. She kept her pace even, but raw emotion was in her expression when her eyes met mine. "I forgot how good running makes me feel. Thank you for dragging me out here. Or threatening to, anyway." Her smile was about the most beautiful thing I'd ever seen.

"You're welcome." It felt good to know I'd brought her some joy. Maybe I did have a bit of a hero complex, but was that so bad? I wasn't seeking glory or recognition. Neither had ever been important to me. I just liked making others feel good. The very first time I'd used a chainsaw on a fallen log had been right after my father was injured. Scared that he wouldn't come home to us, my siblings had needed something to distract them. I'd dragged them outside and bragged that I could carve a knee-high bear with my chainsaw. For a first attempt, I have to say it hadn't turned out that bad, but what mattered more was that painting it and creating the welcome home sign for it to hold had given my siblings something to think about. And that had been good for all of us.

Over the next year, in a show of support, most of the people in Driverton had commissioned a carving from me and, with practice, I became more skilled. Word spread to surrounding towns and before I knew it, I had a steady stream of income from selling everything from ornate benches to life-sized animal lawn ornaments. People purchased them for special occasions, but many contacted me even years later to say how much they still enjoyed them. I'd made a fair share of mistakes in my life, but knowing that something I'd done had made the world a better place—even if only in the tiniest way—made it easier to look myself in the mirror every morning.

Helping Shelby felt a lot like carving that first log had. Did I know what I was doing? Absolutely not, but life had taught me when I did something with good intentions, even when it didn't turn out the way I'd hoped it would, I didn't regret it.

"Let's see what you've got left." I challenged Shelby by taking off down the path, leaving her to chase me this time. Every once in a while, I glanced back to check that she was still with me, but I didn't slow.

We were both dripping with sweat and breathing heavily when we finally made it back to the bed-and-breakfast. Mr. and Mrs. Allen waved to us from the porch as we approached. Shelby and I stopped, side by side, at the bottom of the steps.

Mrs. Allen said, "Well, you two look like you had a good workout."

Shelby glanced at me and smiled. "We did."

Running helped me clear my head. My gut had told me it would be the same for her and I loved the overall glow it had given her. "Let's take a shower."

Her eyes widened.

I chuckled and added, "Separately. Then meet for breakfast. I booked time at a gun range. You can show me how good of a shot you are."

"I've never held a gun."

"Then this will be fun."

"Or interesting. My arms already feel like jelly."

I made the mistake of running a hand down one of them. My intention had been to comfort her, but heat seared through me as I imagined her hot little body sweaty from coming again and again into my mouth. "You'll be fine," I said in a strangled voice.

Her lashes lowered and she inhaled as if she, too, were picturing the two of us together. "I'm not complaining, just want you to be prepared that I might require some instruction."

"I'll teach you anything you want to know." My hand tightened around her arm. I wanted to taste every inch of her, then come with those full lips of hers around my cock. Time stilled, her mouth parted ever so slightly, and I knew my life would never be the same. She would be mine. Maybe not that day, but soon. I could tell myself we'd take things slowly, but no one had ever made me feel so close to losing control.

After a moment, she said, "I've come to a decision."

Nothing beyond her mattered. "Yes?"

"I'm in. Not just for today, but for the whole training program. I need this."

I fought to remain composed. *Yes!* "Good."

She nodded. "This is the best I've felt in—too long. You won't be sorry you took a chance on me. I don't care that the jobs don't pay much or that I'll have to prove myself. I've been thinking, and finding runaways and helping them get home is exactly the kind of challenge I need to get my old confidence back."

Although I was happy to hear that she'd decided to train with me, actually having her take on the kinds of jobs I did with Bradford was out of the question. I'd never let her put herself in that kind of danger. If I held to the plan, though, by the time we got to that point, she wouldn't care. Once she was stronger and feeling better about herself, she'd be so grateful that she'd forgive that little white lie.

I released her arm and let her walk up the steps before me because I'm a gentleman, though I might have used that opportunity to take in that amazing ass of hers once or twice. She stopped midway and glanced back. I shamelessly grinned at her. She quickly looked away and I laughed. We were both doing a piss-poor job at hiding how affected we were by each other.

A few hours later, standing behind Shelby at an indoor firing range, I waited until she'd finished a clip before I put a hand on her shoulder and motioned for her to place the gun down. She did so, then removed her ear protection. I pressed the return button for her target.

She pursed her lips as she watched the hanging paper approach. "Don't say it."

"What?" I asked with humor.

"I'm perfectly aware that I was supposed to aim for the center of the target."

"Or any section of it."

She turned toward me and folded her arms across her chest. "I told you I'd never done this before and that my arms were shaky."

"You did." I cleared my throat. "I didn't realize how serious you were."

A corner of her mouth lifted as if she were fighting back a smile. "Aren't you supposed to encourage me? Build up my confidence?"

"You're right. Let's focus on the positive. You had a good stance and stood in the direction of the target. That's a start."

"Um-hm."

"We don't need to hang a new target which saves on paper and is good for the environment. So, there's that."

"This is where it would be nice if you said you were also awful on your first day at the gun range."

"Me? I was born shooting soda cans off fences with my friends."

Her hands went to her hips. "Okay, hotshot. Show me how it's done."

I sent the target back and put my ear protection on. She did as well. As soon as the target was in place, I unloaded the gun and shot a nice tight grouping. When done, I released the magazine, replaced the gun on the stand before me and pressed the button for the target to return. After removing my headphones, I didn't attempt to hold back my grin as I joked, "Notice how I shot for the inner circle and not the white border around the target."

She handed me her headphones. "Thank you for pointing that out. I couldn't see the target because your big head was in the way."

"That would hurt if I didn't know how into me you are."

Her lashes swept down and she peered at me from beneath them. "You're pretty cocky for someone with a Hulk figurine collection."

I barked out a laugh and my mouth rounded in surprise. "Ouch. That cuts deep. I thought you were sweet."

A slow smile spread across her face. "Then you have a lot to learn about me. We're coming back here tomorrow morning when my arms aren't all wiggly and you're going to teach me how to shoot better than I did today."

Pleasure swept through me. This was what I'd wanted to bring out in her. The rest could wait. "You're on."

Chapter Thirteen

Shelby

A WEEK LATER, I was lying in my bed, exhausted but happy when I received a text from Megan. **You up?**

I am.

How did today go?

Even better than yesterday. We ran eight miles, I shot a tight pattern, and today I learned how to deliver a powerful elbow strike. Did you know that it's safer than punching someone? An elbow packs a lot of power and, in close-contact combat, is more effective than a fist.

I love that you're becoming a badass street fighter.

I laughed. **I'm far from that, but I am beginning to feel like I could protect myself if I had to.**

I didn't know what to think of Everette when you first told me about him, but he's been good for you.

Yes, he has.

I can't believe you haven't slept with him yet.

Hey. It's only been a week.

I know, but I've never seen you this into someone. Is he still helping you with your chin-ups?

I laughed. **Not as much. It's only occasionally that I need his big, strong hands on me . . .**

She sent back a laughing emoji. **I'd be faking a limp and having that hunk of a man carry my ass everywhere.**

I've considered that, I joked. Megan and I didn't have secrets from each other. I told her more than I'd ever put into any journal. **It is tempting to take things further with him, but I don't want to complicate things. Everette makes me feel—hopeful.**

You're going to make me cry.

Stop. I'm serious. I'm definitely attracted to him, but it's deeper than that. He makes me feel empowered. Like I can do anything I set my mind to. I'm confident I can pass whatever test they give me.

Who are THEY?

I don't know yet. Everette said it's not a government agency.

That's the only part that still concerns me. I want all of this for you, but I also want you to be safe.

I sat up. **Safe? Is that even possible? Look at what happened to my parents and they were in their own home. No one is safe.**

My phone rang. Megan only switched from texting to calling when she was worried about me. As soon as I answered, I said, "I'm fine, Megan. All I'm saying is that I'm done being scared. Anything could happen to any of us at any time. Does that mean that we should all hide in bunkers and fear for our lives? That's not living. I've slept with a baseball bat since what happened to my parents, but I was still afraid. I couldn't imagine myself ever actually using it."

"I know."

"I don't feel helpless anymore. I still have the bat, but if someone came in right now—broke down the door and walked in—I'd attack them with everything in me. Maybe I'd win. Maybe I'd lose, but I'm not afraid of the fight anymore."

"It sounds like Everette is giving you something you need, but be careful. There's a lot we don't know about him. What does he say when you ask him where he's from?"

I sighed. "Not much. I can't know any of that until I've proven myself."

"I don't like the sound of that."

"Mr. and Mrs. Allen don't have a problem with him. They've both spoken to his parents."

"That's odd too. Isn't it?"

"I don't think so."

"Are you sure they don't know him better than they've said?"

Her concern was beginning to irritate me. "Megan, I've finally found something that makes me feel good about myself. I don't want to be rude, but can we stop dissecting it? Jeff was a mistake, but one I needed at the time. Maybe it'll turn out that Everette isn't who he says he is, but I can't go back to feeling paralyzed in my head. Things are finally going right for me."

"I'm sorry. I'm not trying to be negative. I love you and I worry."

My irritation fell away. "I'm okay—more okay than I've been in a long time." After a beat, I asked, "How are things with you?"

"Same old, same old. Nothing as exciting as what you're doing. I've been worried about you, but honestly my life isn't a shining example of success. All I seem to do is work, come home, and try to find something to fill my time before I have to go back to work. I'm just existing. My mom says I need a vacation."

"How long have you felt this way?" I'd been in survival mode since losing my parents and it was disconcerting to think Megan had given me unwavering support, but I hadn't realized that she might need me as well.

"For a while. Nothing has been the same since you left."

We'd been a large part of each other's lives for so long—I could see that my withdrawal would have been hard on her. "You've been my rock through all this. I never once asked you what you might need. I can come home for a visit if that would help."

She sniffed. "You really are back."

I smiled. "I think so. Yes."

"Does Everette have a brother?" she joked.

"One, but he's younger and still in college. Who knows, though, he might have a hunky friend in that mysterious town of his."

"It probably wouldn't be that hard to find out where he's from. Do you want me to look into it? With his name and a photo of him it should be easy enough to find that information online. Do you want me to try?"

"No. If he's a scammer, I have nothing for him to take. If he's dangerous, it's a little odd that he's teaching me how to defend myself against him."

"He could be married."

That was something that had crossed my mind a time or

two. "And that would obviously be a deal breaker, but for now I'm choosing to believe him—believe *in* him—and he says he's single. I've been training with him for a week and every day he encourages me to believe in myself more. I'm at the point where if he's running a commune, I'm not so sure I won't join it."

"That's a little scary."

"Don't worry that was one hundred percent . . . well, at least seventy-five percent a joke. I'm sleeping better and feeling good in my own body. Today I woke up smiling. If this all goes south, I can't imagine feeling helpless again. This week brought out sides of me I'd forgotten I had. I love challenges and I'm naturally competitive."

"Yes, you are."

"I can focus and persevere. Physical pain doesn't scare me. It never did. I don't know why I let myself get so afraid."

"You had people you love torn away from you. That would shake up anyone."

"I let all of it get in my head and shut me down. I don't go on social media so why should I care what a bunch of strangers think of me? And anyone who seeks me out thinking they have the right to say something rude to me? I have every right to tell them where they can shove their opinions of me."

"Okay, you sold it; if Everette is running a commune, I'm joining with you."

"At least we'd be together," I said lightly.

"I do miss that."

I let out a sigh. "Me too. I'd suggest you come here,

but—"

She laughed. "No, enjoy this time with Everette. Something tells me you'll soon be having the best sex of your life and I'll be living vicariously through you."

"Until I meet his friends and find the perfect one for you."

"Sounds like a plan."

Chapter Fourteen

Everette

T HE SUN HAD just come up when I grabbed my phone and was about to head down to meet Shelby, but decided to make a quick call. The first step of my plan to help Shelby was complete. It was time to move to step two.

Bradford answered with, "What do you need?"

"Has everyone rehearsed what they'll say when they meet Shelby?"

"No idea," Bradford said in an irritated tone that had my antennae going up.

"You've been training them, right?"

"Let's just say they're not as *dedicated* to the process as you were."

That news wasn't surprising, but it was disappointing. Certain lifestyles were hard to escape. If you weren't careful, like a quicksand pit, the more you tried to escape them the more they could pull you back in. "What did they do?"

"They were late on the first day, half-assed their way through every task I gave them, then celebrated what they considered an achievement with a few rounds of beer. Katie got frustrated with them so she also quit. I don't have time for their shit."

"Don't give up on them, Bradford. I've known Levi and Ollie my whole life. If they're fucking up it's because they're afraid to fail. I had to conquer that hurdle myself. It's easy to believe you're not capable of more than where you are and what you've known."

"They're grown men and I'm not a babysitter."

"I'll talk to them."

"Do what you want. They're nice enough people, but they'd need to prove themselves worth my time before I gave them a second chance."

Fuck. "If they're drinking, I can't trust them to follow the plan we came up with."

"How's Shelby doing?"

"Fantastic. You should see the difference in her. She looks me straight in the eye now. I'm scaffolding the workouts with her the same as you did with me. We do a little more every day. And she's actually a pretty good shot now. Her confidence is through the roof."

"Sounds like you don't need anyone's help. Just keep doing what you're doing."

"I told Shelby she'd be tested. I don't want to tell her that—"

"You lied?"

"I didn't . . . Okay, technically I lied about her being able to work with us, but she'll only be pissed with me if I tell her that now. When you trained me, you told me to trust the process. I've put a lot of thought into each step of this.

I've earned her trust. She's learning how not to be afraid anymore. It's important for her to have a win also. Ollie and Levi probably need the same thing, but I can only help one person at a time. She needs to think she's stumbled upon clues, found someone on her own, and made a difference. That's what will cement her confidence that she's capable of so much more. She needs this."

"She's not going to be happy with you when she finds out."

"I disagree. When she sees how much planning went into this and she meets Tyr, there's no way she'll be able to stay upset."

"Good luck with that."

"Don't say that like you're not involved. I need your help now more than before. If Ollie, Levi, and Katie are out, I need someone to play the roles they were going to."

"I'm not letting Joanna get involved in this."

"There's no danger. It's a made-up case."

"No."

"And she'd be helping someone who has survived significant trauma. You can't tell me she wouldn't love to be a part of that." Bradford's wife ran a rescue for mini-horses. If there was anyone with a bigger heart when it came to helping, I'd never met them.

"Ask Cooper for help."

"I can't. He's too close to Levi and Ollie. They'd never forgive me for involving him and not them. I need someone a little removed from Driverton."

"Why do you think I know anyone who has time for

something like this?"

"You have to know someone."

The half-laugh Bradford let out made me question if I hadn't made a mistake by pushing him to help. "I do know one person who would eat something like this up."

I didn't have much of a choice, not if I wanted to push forward with my plan. "Who?"

"Clay Landon."

"Cooper's rich older brother?"

"That's him."

"I've met him a few times, but I couldn't ask him for something like this."

"Trust me, he's bored and this is exactly the kind of thing he loves. He calls himself a fairy godfather extraordinaire."

"Could he hold to an alias? Would he take it seriously? This isn't a joke to me."

"I'll talk to him. His wife would probably enjoy it too."

"We originally planned for three people."

Bradford made a sound akin to a growl. "I'll fucking ask Joanna."

"Thanks. And I still need you to be—you. All you have to do is come here, say you need to speak to me, and give us a rundown on the case."

"Fine. When?"

"Tomorrow?"

"I'll be there."

"Hey, Bradford, I appreciate it. And when you meet Shelby, you'll understand why this is so important to me."

"You've got it pretty bad for her?"

"I do. Right now, that's not my focus, though. She was lost when I found her. Locate, retrieve, return home: that's what I've learned from you—that's what I'm determined to do for her."

"And if that home isn't with you?"

I'd considered that. "I'll still know I did the right thing. She was sinking, Bradford. There's a sparkle in her eyes again. No matter how this turns out, I did that."

"If I ever do give Levi and Ollie a second chance, it'll only be because you're too fucking nice of a person to say no to."

I laughed at that. "I'll remember that." After checking the time on my watch, I said, "Shit. I'm late. See you tomorrow."

Chapter Fifteen

Shelby

THERE WAS A spring to my step as I made my way down to breakfast. Mrs. Allen had replaced her usual spread with a protein shake that didn't weigh us down but gave Everette and me enough of a boost to start our day.

Not seeing Everette already in the dining room with both of our drinks surprised me. I headed into the kitchen. Mrs. Allen looked up from rinsing out a blender in the sink. "Well, look at you. I swear you get prettier every day you're here."

I blushed and fought back a strong desire to hug her. "Not sure about prettier, but happier—definitely. I'm filling up that journal you gave me and it feels good."

She nodded toward the full glasses on the island between us. "I'm sure that has nothing to do with the company you're keeping."

"I have no idea what you're talking about." Smiling, I leaned forward and picked up both drinks. For once, I'd be the one smugly sitting at the dining room table pretending I'd been waiting there forever.

"Um-hmm." She wiped her hands on a towel then leaned back against the sink. "On that note, I'm glad we have a moment alone. There's something I need to ask you."

Her expression was so serious, I replaced both drinks on the island. "Sure. Anything." No matter what she asked of me it wouldn't make a dent in how much I owed her for the kindness she'd shown me.

"Drew received a call from his brother this morning. He lives on his own and fell down the stairs."

"Oh, my God."

"He'll be fine, but he fractured a bone in his foot and needs someone to help him get around for a few days. Normally we would close up this house and just go, but I feel comfortable with you and Everette staying here without us if you're okay with that."

"Me and Everette," I whispered. "Alone."

"If you have any reservations about that, I can stay, and Drew can take care of his brother without me."

Imagining how quickly things might progress without the Allens there, a rush of heat flooded through me. "No, we'll be fine," I squeaked out.

She chuckled. "That's what I thought. You have our contact information. If you need anything, we'll only be a few hours away. Obviously, you'll have to start making your own meals and we'll give you a discount on the nightly rate."

I shook my head. "Please don't. You've already been so generous—"

"While we're gone, think of this like a whole house rental. Eat whatever food is here. Use whatever appliances or anything you need. I'm not sure how long we'll be gone, but I'm thinking at least a week."

"A week." *Oh, yes.*

"Unless you need us back before then."

"No. No. It's all good."

"I'm sure it will be." I wasn't bold enough to address the knowing look in her eyes.

"When do you leave?"

"This morning. Drew is already packing."

Everette chose that moment to show up at the door of the kitchen. "Morning."

Mrs. Allen waved to Everette. "I'd stay and explain what's going on, but I don't trust Drew to know what to pack for me. We'll be gone before you get back for lunch."

"Gone?" Everette asked with a frown. "Is everything okay?"

"Shelby will fill you in." She moved away from the sink and started for the other door to the kitchen, then paused and pinned us each with a look. "Be good to each other while we're gone."

"We will," I promised like a child being left alone for the afternoon for the first time. After Mrs. Allen's departure, I couldn't quite bring myself to look Everette in the eye. Instead, I sought a spoon to mix the drinks.

"What did I miss?" Everette asked.

Keeping my attention on fiddling with the drinks, I said, "Mr. Allen's brother fractured his foot and needs someone there. Mr. and Mrs. Allen are heading out this morning to stay with him. They think for about a week."

"A week." Everette cleared his throat.

"Yes. They asked if we were okay being here alone."

"And you said?"

I looked up, desire searing through me when our eyes met. How I answered him would very likely determine how the next week went. I'd told myself I didn't want to complicate everything by taking things to the next level, but this was an opportunity I hadn't expected. Part of me wanted to play it cool and let him set the pace. Part of me wanted to not waste a single moment of the time alone we'd just been gifted. Letting out a shaky breath, I said, "I told her we'd be fine."

He stepped closer until only the small kitchen island was between us. "And is that how you feel? If you're uncomfortable with this at all, I can find a nearby place to stay or you can invite your friend Megan to come here. I want you to know that—"

What a good man. I interrupted whatever else he would have said by grabbing the neck of his shirt and pulling him forward over the island and claiming his mouth with mine. It was a brief, but passionate kiss that ended with me hastily releasing him and taking an embarrassed step back.

A myriad of expressions crossed his face—surprise, desire, pleasure. As he straightened, a slow grin spread across his face. "Okay then."

Breathing heavily, I said, "All week you've been telling me to be clear and decisive."

His face went delightfully pink. "That's what I said."

I squared my shoulders and looked him in the eye. "This

is me being both." When he didn't immediately answer I started to worry that my directness had made him uncomfortable. "Did—did I—are you . . ." Embarrassment battled with concern for him. He'd been so good to me. Maybe he was married and had changed his mind about being able to cheat on his wife. If he announced that now, could I even be angry with him? Sure I'd be hurt. And, yes, disappointed that he'd lied to me. But Everette was the reason I was no longer waking up dreading the day ahead of me. "Listen, if you're married with kids, or even just married, nothing has happened between us but it's time for you to go back to them. I'm in a much better place than where you found me. And whatever is wrong back there, if you bring the positive energy that you've shown me back to them—it'll make a difference."

"No children. No wife."

I swallowed hard. "Fiancée? Girlfriend?"

"Neither."

"Oh." He was attracted to me. A week ago, he'd talked about how he would want to be with me when I was ready. Well, I was ready. "I'm confused. I thought—"

"You thought right." With that, he smirked and walked to me. His eyes stayed riveted to mine. His hands cupped my shoulders then slid slowly, tantalizingly down my arms. "I've been telling myself all week to not rush you."

"I don't feel rushed," I breathed.

His head dropped closer, erasing any embarrassment I had. My body hummed for his. Every place our bodies weren't touching was torture. I moved closer, writhing against him, needing to feel more of him against me. He gathered me closer, his excitement hard and proud against my stomach. "Too short," he muttered, easily lifting me so my ass balanced on the edge of the island. One more adjustment, and there was only him and the thrill of being wrapped around him. "There, that's better."

It was. It really was. My only response was a nod. I'd imagined this so many times, even dreamed it more than once. Would the reality of him live up to my fantasy? God, I hoped so.

Holding me to him with one hand, he dug his other into my hair and angled my head upward. "Promise me something."

There was nothing I would have refused him in that moment. Wide-eyed and so turned on I could barely think straight, I bit my bottom lip and nodded again.

His hand tightened on my hair until my lips parted in a gasp. "Don't give me the woman you think I want. Be as real and as bold with this as I've seen you become with everything else. I can wait if you need more time, but once we open this door, I'm all in. Are you ready for that?"

My tongue darted across my bottom lip. "I don't know what that means."

His eyes grazed over my face possessively and his hand tightened on my ass. "I'm not looking for a casual fuck. That's not who I am anymore. It's not what I want to be to you." His lips brushed over mine in a tease that mesmerized me. His scent, his strength, his hunger for me overwhelmed my senses. The need within me was not the slow-building desire I was accustomed to with other men. Comparing Everette to them was like trying to compare the flames contained in a fireplace to those that ravaged a forest. One was pleasant, the other too wild to be controlled. "Say you're mine, and we'll take our training sessions indoors."

Training sessions? I swallowed hard. "Training sessions?"

His grin was all dare. "Scared? Of me? I thought the fierce woman who used a leg sweep to knock me on my ass yesterday would be a little bolder. You don't like some-thing—say it. You want something—take it. That's what I'm talking about. Don't fuck me halfway. Use your voice as well as that gorgeous mouth of yours. Tell me what you like, what you've always wanted to try, and what you don't want. I don't want less than that, because I sure as hell am going to teach you what I want. Would you like it if we both brought that kind of realness to this?"

"Yes. Yes, I would."

"Then say it. Say you're mine."

A wave of confidence rolled through me. "I'm yours, and Everette—"

"Yes?"

"You're mine." I laced both of my hands behind his neck and brought his mouth down to mine. There was a thrill in submitting to him that was matched by how exciting it was to claim him. His strength surrounded me and giving myself over to it, knowing that he was giving himself over to me, was intoxicating.

There was no hesitation to how he drove his tongue through my lips to deepen the kiss. His tongue encircled mine, drawing it into an intimate dance full of the promise of more. I opened to him, arching so my sex could brush impatiently over his steely bulge. He easily positioned me to give me better access and I ground myself harder against him.

"I told you we didn't need to say goodbye to them," Mrs. Allen said from somewhere in the distance. "Does it look like they're worried about us?"

Everette's head whipped away from mine and he gently, but quickly, returned me to standing before him. We both turned to face the older couple. Everette said, "Sorry about that."

Frowning, Mr. Allen pinned Everette with a long look. "You're both adults, it's none of my business what happens here while we're away. Clean up after yourselves and, Everette, I have your parents' number. Don't give me a reason to use it."

"I will. I mean, I won't give you a reason to call them, but we'll make sure we keep the house in order."

Everette sounded so sincere, I felt transported back to the awkward sex talk my parents had when I'd started dating. I let out a nervous laugh which drew Mr. Allen's attention to me.

His frown deepened. "You have our number. If he is anything but respectful, call us."

Mrs. Allen swatted his chest. "Like you said, Drew, they're adults. If respect is all that happens while we're gone, I'll be disappointed in both of them. Now let's go. Your brother is waiting for us and just thinking about what'll be happening in this house has me hoping he's a deep sleeper."

Everette wrapped his arms around me from behind. I felt the rumble of his laughter against my back. "Mr. Allen, you are one lucky man."

Mr. Allen stood taller and glared at Everette. "Say that again and see how many teeth I leave in your pretty boy smile."

Mrs. Allen linked arms with her husband while fanning her face with her free hand. "He talks like that because he knows it turns me on."

The love in Mr. Allen's face when he looked down at his wife confirmed her claim. "Guilty as charged." He nodded toward me then Everette again. "In all seriousness, you both seem like nice enough people. Be good to each other. You only get one shot at the first time. Do it justice." He glanced down at Sandy then added, "And don't break the furniture. It was a damn shame what we did to the chair your grandmother left us."

Everette barked out a laugh that I echoed. "Good-bye," he said cheerfully. "Don't hurry back."

I hugged his arm to my stomach even after we were alone again. Everette nuzzled my neck from behind. "What are you thinking?"

"About your parents. What are they like?"

"That's not where my thoughts were at all—but okay." He hugged me closer. "My mom is a strong, proud, traditional mother. She's strict, but never mean. My father is a quiet man. Proud too. He was a hard worker before his injury that left him in a wheelchair. It was difficult for him to accept help from anyone at first. He hated that my mother had to work and that she worried when she didn't earn enough to cover the bills. I think if someone had told him she'd get a million dollars if he offed himself, he would have back then. In his mind he'd failed as a provider and she deserved better. My mother never saw it that way, but she also didn't know how to bring in enough money to support us and that was humbling for her."

"Which is why you stepped up."

"Yes."

"How did your father handle that?"

"It's been a love/hate experience. He's grateful, but it's not what he wanted for me."

I turned in Everette's arms and looked up into his beautiful eyes. "I'm sure he's proud of who you are."

"Yes and no, but we're getting there. In some ways I grew up faster than I should have. In others, I dragged my feet a little."

"What does he think of your side job?"

"He doesn't know about it. If he did, he wouldn't approve because it can be dangerous. Technically, I'm the man of the house for now. If anything happened to me—"

I laid my fingers gently over his lips. "Don't say another word or I might do something stupid like fall for you."

He kissed my fingers then moved my hand from his mouth to his chest. "And we wouldn't want that, would we?"

"Not before I know if you're any good in bed," I joked.

His laugh started in his eyes then spilled out. "You're a practical woman. I can respect that."

"If respect is all that happens while the Allens are gone, I'll be disappointed too," I murmured. With the men I'd been with in the past I would never have been bold the way I felt I could be with Everette. He'd told me not to do this halfway and that was freeing.

"Remember all those moves I taught you this week?"

"Yes."

His hands moved to my waist. "Don't use them this week." With that he lifted me the way he'd done during our first day of training and tossed me over his shoulder. "I have a few fantasies to act out with you and none of them involve a trip to the ER."

Carrying me as if I weighed nothing, Everette headed out of the kitchen and up the stairs toward our bedrooms.

I laughed against his back. "If this is one of them, I'm pretty sure we're on the same page. I've been thinking about this all week."

He kicked his slightly ajar door open. "Me too."

Without warning he tossed me on the bed, then came to stand beside it. The laughter was gone from his eyes—replaced by the same fire that was burning through me. "Stand up on the bed and strip for me."

I rose to my knees then to my feet. The only thing that stopped me from feeling ridiculous as I stepped out of my running shoes and socks was the intensity of his gaze. I dropped them to the floor.

"Keep going," he said in a deep, husky tone that no woman would have refused. Holding on to the hem on both sides, I swept my T-shirt up and over my head, dropping it beside my shoes. My sports bra came off with a less graceful move, but he didn't seem to mind when that hit the floor as well.

His hands came up to cup my small breasts. "You're so fucking beautiful."

I felt beautiful. "You're not so bad yourself."

With one hand moving to my lower back, he pulled me closer, then bent and took one of my breasts into his mouth, circling his tongue around my hard nipple. "I want to see all of you," he murmured as he kissed his way across to my other breast.

No further encouragement was needed for me to shimmy out of both my biker shorts and panties at the same time. He raised his head and took a step back, looking me over from head to toe, taking his time. "Everything looks so good. Where should I start?"

It could have been a rhetorical question, but I choked out, "On your knees."

The sound he emitted was somewhere between a growl and a purr. "I love that you know what you want, but let's meet halfway. Spread your legs for me."

Holding his gaze, I did.

"Show me how you touch yourself when no one's around."

I brought my hand to my sex and slid a finger between my folds. Wet and eager for him, I settled a finger on my clit and began to stroke it. Never had I been confident enough in my sexuality to please myself while someone watched, but it was exciting. His eyes darkened as he watched me.

He bent, took one of my nipples between his teeth and gave it a gentle tug. I nearly came from that alone. As if sensing that, he repeated the move on my other breast. When he raised his head, I was breathing heavily and rubbing myself faster.

"Dip a finger inside yourself."

I did as he ordered and it felt so fucking good.

"I want to taste you," he said.

Withdrawing my finger, I brought it to his mouth. He circled it with his tongue. "Oh, that's good," he growled. "Too good for just a sample."

Wrapping his hands around each of my ankles, he pulled my feet out from under me, sending me falling back onto the bed. I shrieked, but from surprise rather than fear. In one powerful move he hauled me to the edge of the bed, spread my legs wide for him and claimed my sex with his mouth.

His tongue was as bold as it was large. It swept over me from front to back, then plunged into me. With talented fingers he parted my folds and began to work my clit with his fingers while his tongue seared me to my very soul.

I gripped the blanket on either side of me and bucked against his mouth. There was no hesitation in his plundering, no mercy. I was his to take and he knew it. Had someone asked me before Everette if I made noise during sex, I would have said I didn't. But there I was calling out his name, begging for him to not stop. And when he didn't, I dug my hands into his hair, held his face to my sex and came so hard I thought I might die.

"Good girl," he said as he raised his face and wiped my

juices from around his mouth. "My turn. Get up."

Still reeling from the glow of my orgasm, I rolled up on-to my knees, bringing me face-to-face with his cock that was tenting his running shorts. He stepped out of his socks and running shoes and was about to slide his shorts down when I stopped him.

"Let me do it," I said breathlessly and moved to sit on the edge of the bed before him. His cock sprung free, huge and hard, as soon as the material cleared it. I tossed his shorts on the pile of my own clothing. Nothing about Everette was small. I took a moment to appreciate the sheer size of him.

"Take me in your mouth. All in."

My eyes widened, unsure if that was possible, but I didn't want to disappoint. Cupping his balls with one hand, I opened my mouth and took him in. I half expected him to thrust himself down my throat, but he didn't.

He must have felt me bracing myself for that because his hands ran through my hair and he whispered, "You feel so fucking good."

I circled his cock with my tongue and took him deeper and deeper, so deep I was afraid I might gag, but I didn't because he let me choose my rhythm and my comfort. When I began to move up and down on him, his hands fisted in my hair, but still he didn't move. I got bolder, better, and began to experiment with exactly what drove him wild.

He groaned and adjusted his stance, giving me an even better angle. I worked my lips and tongue up and down his shaft, teasing, sucking, drawing him deeper still.

"I'm going to come," he grunted.

I could have pulled back, but I didn't. My response was to suckle on him even harder, which he took as a sign to continue. He held my head and thrust forward, spilling deep into my throat. I swallowed it all.

When he withdrew, I was shaking, feeling nearly as shattered by his orgasm as I had been by mine. He offered me a hand, hauled me to my feet then placed me back on the bed but this time facing away from him. He ran his hands down the outside of my legs then moved them so they were farther apart and caressed the inside from ankle to sex.

His teeth nipped at my butt cheeks. "I've wanted to do this all week. Your ass is perfect."

"Thank you?" I was nearly incoherent with need.

As his mouth continued to explore me from behind, his hands were everywhere at once. From behind, he thrust two fingers upward into my sex and began to pump in and out. His other hand brought a rhythmic frontal assault to my clit. I gasped and tried to remain steady on my feet. That talented tongue of his tasted every inch of me until I was making all kinds of wild sounds again. The spot that was a mystery to some men was not to him. When his fingers rolled over it again and again I clenched around them and cried out for him to not stop.

I nearly wept when he did.

But the sound of a condom wrapper being opened had anticipation replacing disappointment. He turned me ever so slowly back toward him. Gloriously fully erect again and sheathed for me, his cock was a temptation I couldn't resist. It twitched beneath my light touch.

"Come here," Everette growled.

I took his hand and let him guide me to the edge of the bed again. This time he eased me down onto it. We kissed deeply, a primal blending of our flavors, before he pushed me backward until I was lying half on the bed, with my feet on the floor.

He slid his hands beneath my knees and hauled me even more off the bed. I wrapped my legs around his waist and the tip of his cock nudged against my wet folds. One of his hands moved beneath my ass to support my weight. His other hand ran up and down my stomach, with his thumb stopping now and then to roll across my clit.

When he entered me, it was with one deep, powerful thrust that filled me so completely it hurt a little. I bit my lip as my body stretched to accommodate him. I arched my back more, taking him deeper. He gave my ass a smack from beneath and my legs widened even more. He withdrew almost completely, then thrust deeply into me again. My eyes rolled back in my head from the pleasure of it. And it was just the beginning.

All gentleness left him as he began to pound into me. All I could do was hold on to the bed and let go of any illusion of being in control. It was more than sex; it was a primal claiming. I'd never felt that I belonged to a man or even realized what that meant, but in the wildness of our mating, when I couldn't get enough of him and he couldn't get enough of me, I understood the universe and my purpose in it. Everything that had never made sense suddenly did and tears filled my eyes.

He stopped. "Are you okay?"

"Don't you dare fucking stop," I growled.

I didn't need to say that twice. I called out his name, told him how fucking good he felt, and announced to probably every house within a mile that I was coming. He continued to pound into me even after I climaxed, then joined me with one final thrust and a swear.

When he withdrew and removed the condom, I shifted backward so I was more on the bed. He was beside me in a heartbeat, pulling me up and then settling me against one muscled side of him. "That was a good start," he said, kissing my forehead.

"Start?" I choked on the word and a laugh.

"Shh," he said in an amused tone. "In my fantasy you talked less."

I gave his side a playful pinch. "Jerk."

He chuckled. "And there was no pinching."

"Well, in my fantasy you were charming."

"Like creepy kissing you while you sleep charming? Or as charming as the prince who couldn't remember who he'd spent the ball dancing with?"

Running my hand over his broad chest, I smiled up at him. "You watched fairy tales?"

"Against my will. I have a younger sister who used to love them."

I snuggled closer to him. "You're a man of many layers and surprises."

He clapped a hand on one of my buttocks. "You have no idea."

I lifted my head again, hoping he'd elaborate on that, but he didn't, and honestly, I was too sated to care. I reached behind me, grabbed a corner of the blanket and pulled it over us. My breathing slowed to match his and I slipped away into a post-sex nap.

Chapter Sixteen

Everette

LATER THAT DAY, on a sandy lakeside beach, Shelby and I were soaking up some sun on a blanket. I had one arm folded beneath my head and the other around her. Her hair was loose and tickling my side, but I didn't mind. We'd replaced our morning run with another hour of exploring each other. Sharp shooting practice? We'd used that time for a long shower and a leisurely lunch. Currently we were in our bathing suits, cuddling between swims rather than working on self-defense techniques.

"Everette?"

"Mmm?"

"You know a lot about what I've been struggling with, but tell me something that you worry about."

I shrugged. "There's nothing, really."

She propped herself up on one elbow and looked down at me. "I do that."

"What?"

"I say everything is fine when it isn't."

I kissed her shoulder. "I'm here with you. What could I

be worried about?"

She frowned. "Maybe nothing. I was just thinking about what you said this morning in the kitchen. You talked about not wanting to do this halfway. I know you were referring to the sex, but I want to be that real when it comes to getting to know each other."

Unsure what she was hoping I'd say, I simply looked at her and waited.

Her lips pursed as she seemed to choose how to best explain her request to me. "I'll go first. I pride myself on being independent and strong, so when I fall apart, I'm ashamed. I don't want to put the burden of my issues on anyone. I tell everyone I'm okay because I feel like I should be able to handle it on my own." She splayed a hand across my chest. "Then you came along and pushed me until I admitted the truth. I resented the help at first, but it was what I needed."

Running my hand gently through her hair, I weighed what she was saying as well as what it meant she wanted from me. "There were a lot of things that used to scare or frustrate me and none of them felt within my control. I didn't know if I could make an income that could support my family without leaving my small town. I learned to plow forward without putting too much thought into how I felt about anything. So, is there anything I'm worried about? I don't know. I don't allow myself to stop and think about how things could go wrong. Until this past year, I achieved that level of Zen through alcohol. I've replaced that with working out and setting goals for myself."

She relaxed back onto my shoulder. "That sounds like a

healthy choice."

"For me it has been."

Glancing up at me, she lightly slapped my chest. "See, right there, unless I'm completely wrong at reading your mood—there's something bothering you. Are you missing partying with your friends?"

"The opposite. I'm worried about them—"

"Aha! I knew it. You *are* worried about something."

Impressive. Her instinct for uncovering the truth was as good as Mrs. Allen's. Or I really was a horrible liar. "I am. I feel like I've opened a whole new chapter of my life—one full of endless possibilities—and they could as well. But they don't want to."

"Or they're not ready to."

I nuzzled the top of her head. "Or they're not ready to."

She snuggled closer and sighed. "Tell me something about them. Do they work on top secret side jobs too?"

"Ollie and Levi? No. It'd be nice to see them step up and join in, but right now they're not taking anything seriously enough. Remember the man I told you had trained me?"

"Bradford?"

"Yes. He offered to train them as well. They didn't make it past the first day."

"That's a shame."

"It really is because I know they would be so good at it. Ollie has a natural way with people. They not only trust him, but he inspires loyalty. When he took over his father's pub, it was in financial trouble. It should have gone under. Had anyone else taken it over, it would have. But when Ollie couldn't afford to buy food for the kitchen, people rallied and raised money so he could. Hell, there are still things on the menu that people cook at home and bring in as donations."

"What do you bring?"

"The best beef jerky in the northeast. According to my father, our recipe has been passed down in my family for five generations. People who try it for the first time always ask for the recipe, but I promised my father that only my children will get that from me."

She raised her head to look me in the eye again. "You have children?"

"Not yet."

Her forehead wrinkled. "You want children?"

"Of course I do." Interesting. "Don't you?"

She took a moment before answering. "I used to imagine myself with a family, but I don't know anymore. I don't think I could survive losing another person I love."

That tugged at my heart. "That's the worst-case scenario and I don't allow myself to imagine those. Lightning happens and I'm sure it kills, but I don't let that stop me from enjoying a storm now and then."

She nodded. "I recently said something similar to Megan regarding you."

"Me?"

"She was worried about all the things we don't know about you. She doesn't want to see me get hurt."

"And what did you say?"

"I told her my parents died in their own home—a place

that should have been safe. They followed all the rules, were good people, worked hard, were kind to strangers, and careful when it came to watching over me. If something bad could happen to them, safety is nothing more than an illusion. So, although being with you is risky . . . I don't want to live in a state of constant fear."

Cupping her face with one hand, I guided her mouth to mine for a gentle kiss I hoped said everything I didn't know how to put into words. Had I thought either of us was ready for it, I would have declared I'd always protect her. After kissing her, I lay back, tucking her once again to my side. "I'd never intentionally hurt you."

"I believe you."

"And not all secrets are a bad thing. Surprise parties, for example. How fun would they be if the person being surprised knew everything up-front?"

"That's true."

"Ollie's mom, Mrs. Williams, is a well of wisdom—often unsolicited and painfully true, but wise nonetheless. She says that acts of kindness are something best left unspoken. I'm on the fence with that one. On one hand, if you're going to do something for someone, it leaves them with more of their pride if you don't make a big deal out of it. On the other hand, I also believe one act of kindness can inspire others to step up and help. Mrs. Williams is also not above public acts of forced restitution, so there's some ambiguity to her philosophies."

"Forced restitution?"

I told her the story of how she'd handled the teens who'd

partied at Mrs. Tissbury's pond. She laughed with me as I described how everyone in town feared the wrath of Mrs. Williams. Even me.

She asked me for more stories from my town. Without giving away last names, I told her about Cooper and how he'd come to our town to hide from the brutality of certain members of his family. "Some of it we knew, some of it came out only recently. He's partly why I started working with Bradford. Both he and Cooper were out there doing good things that no one will ever read about in the news. They risk their lives on the regular for people they don't know and they do it with no expectation of compensation or recognition. When the opportunity to join them was offered to me, I knew I couldn't turn it down."

"How many children have you helped bring home?"

"Only three so far."

"Only?" She sat up. "That's three more than I have."

I said, "You were why we found Alexia."

She sighed. "I don't count that, but my chance to make a real difference will come because you're giving me the opportunity to do what you do."

"Yeah." I kept my gaze locked on the tranquil water of the lake. There was no way I'd ever consider sending Shelby off to dodge bullets with Bradford. And Cooper? Although he stopped short of leaving carnage in his wake, Cooper still danced on the wrong side of the law. There was zero chance that any of us would allow Shelby to work one of the real jobs that came in. Shaking those thoughts off, I decided to focus on how amazing it was to have Shelby all to myself.

"Want to go for another swim?"

"Sure."

I stood, offered her my hand, and helped her to her feet. I started walking toward the water but stopped immediately when I noticed she wasn't at my side. "You okay?" Her serious expression from before had been replaced by a more playful one. God, she looked hot in that little bikini of hers. And when she bit her bottom lip? I melted.

She pointed to the water and pouted. "The water. It's just so far."

I laughed and returned to her side. "Just because I carried you in last time doesn't mean I'll always carry you. Do I look like your personal transportation device?"

Sporting that sexy little smile of hers, she went up on her tiptoes and murmured, "So, you don't also love when I wrap my arms around your neck, my legs around your waist, and accidentally brush up and down across your dick as you walk? Too bad. You're right, I can get myself to the water."

"Now that you mention it, that water does look too far away for you to walk." When I lifted her off her feet, she wound herself around me, settling her sex over my quickly hardening cock. "Do you know what's even farther?"

"What?" She writhed against me.

I temporarily lost my cool and kissed her deeply, my hands wandering to places they shouldn't have in an area where someone might walk up and see us. When I raised my head, I was panting and ready to take her right then and there. I gained some control, though, and said, "The house. Instead of dinner, what do you say I eat you out on the dining room table?"

She shuddered against me. "That's not wrong, is it?"

"Break nothing. Clean up afterward. That's all I heard for rules." I didn't wait for her to decide—her answer was in the way she tightened her legs around my waist, arched against me, and dug her hands into my back. "Table it is."

Chapter Seventeen

Shelby

W HEN I WOKE in Everette's arms the next morning, I was sore in a different way than I'd been earlier in the week, but smiling just the same. I didn't feel a shred of embarrassment that what we'd started on the dining room table had ended on the wall of the hallway because we'd been too impatient to make it to my bed. If the rest of the week continued this way, I'd need to buy another gratitude journal—or a bookcase of them. And locks. They'd need locks. My list of what I'd become grateful for had taken a spicy turn.

"Why are you awake?" Everette murmured into my hair.

"No run today?" I teased. I could barely walk.

"We could." He groaned. "Or we could stay in today, rest, and double down on working out tomorrow."

I turned in his arms. "Rest? Is that what we're calling it now?"

A sexy laugh rumbled out of him before he gave me the unrushed, warm kiss of a long-time lover. "I'm game for whatever."

The heated look we exchanged, the one that would have led to us starting a whole new session of lovemaking was interrupted by the sound of a loud knock on the front door of the house. I sat straight up and grabbed a sheet to cover myself.

"I'll go see who that is," Everette said, rolling away.

I was off the bed before he was on his feet. "No."

"It's probably a delivery." He stepped into a pair of boxer briefs then jeans. "I'll be right back."

Naked, I planted myself in his path. The sudden panic rising within me was evident in the high pitch of my voice. "Please don't go."

Everette stopped. He pulled on a shirt, gave me an odd look, then compassion filled his eyes. "It's okay, Shelby. You're safe."

I blinked back angry tears as my hands fisted at my sides. "I know." There was another bang on the door that flamed the fear I'd thought I had under control. My anger with myself spilled over in his direction. "Do you think I don't know that? But that doesn't help."

"Okay," he said gently. "What would help? What do you need?"

"I'm going with you." I looked around for my baseball bat and grabbed it. "I need to face this fear head-on."

He nodded slowly. "That's probably a good idea, but if I could make one suggestion?"

"Unless you have a better weapon for me to hold, I'm taking the bat."

I didn't recognize the pained amusement in his eyes for

what it was until he waved a hand at my torso and said, "The bat's fine. I'm just thinking that you might want to put something on. Your choice."

A quick look down confirmed that there was a good chance I'd lost my mind. "I'm naked."

"Yes, you are."

I handed him the bat. "Hold this." In a flash, I threw on a bra, underwear, shorts and a T-shirt. "Ready." I held out my hand for the bat.

He returned it to me reluctantly. "We're in a quiet community. A lot of people around here don't even lock their doors. Let me do the talking. We should find out what the person wants before you start swinging that thing."

I almost snapped at him for doubting how I'd handle the situation, but all things considered, I couldn't blame him for being concerned. I wouldn't have thought an unexpected knock on a door could topple the progress I'd made. "Deal."

As we were walking down the stairs, Everette's phone beeped. He checked it and swore.

"What is it?" I asked in a rush.

"Nothing. I just forgot about something." He stopped and put out an arm to block me. "It's probably better if I answer the door on my own."

"What? Why?"

"Could you just trust me on this one?"

I wanted to. If my emotions weren't already in overdrive maybe I could have. Instead my hands tightened on the bat. "Who's out there?" A horrific thought came to me. "Your wife?"

He bent and looked me in the eye. "I'm not married. And before you ask, no, there's no jealous girlfriend or baby mama either."

"So, who's out there?" When he didn't immediately answer me, I stormed, "I'm trying to respect all of your secrets, but I'm not doing so well with that right now."

He rubbed a hand down his face. "It's a friend of mine."

I wasn't sure I liked that either. "One of your friends from home? Like Levi or Ollie?"

"No. Bradford."

"The man who trained you? The one you say so many good things about?"

"That's him."

"I don't have all day," a male voice boomed from the other side of the door.

A shiver shot down my spine. "He sounds angry."

"That's his normal voice." With a frustrated sound, Everette lowered his arm and started down the steps again.

"What's he doing here?" I asked.

"Hopefully something that has him in a good mood."

I tucked the bat behind me, but stood beside Everette as he opened the door. I gasped as I looked Bradford over. He was an inch or two shorter than Everette, but muscled and scarred like someone who'd visited the bowels of hell and been expelled. There was a coldness in his eyes that had me taking a step back. I would have bet my life that he'd unalived more than one person. This was who Everette worked with? Suddenly all the things I didn't know about Everette and what he did mattered.

When Everette moved closer to put a supportive arm around me, he encountered the bat. His hand closed over it in what was probably an attempt to take it from me. I tightened my grip on it.

He inhaled deeply, seemed to accept my decision, slid his arm around my waist and greeted the man at the door. "Bradford. I meant to call you. There's been a change of plans."

"Too late. Everyone is on board and in place."

"This isn't really a good time."

Bradford looked from Everette to me and back. "I'm not fucking doing this twice."

"I would never ask you to. It's just that the Allens are gone for the week and we promised to watch the house for them."

Rising to his full height, Bradford's expression hardened and he growled, "Are you telling me that I'm here for nothing?"

My body began to shake. I didn't want it to. My brain attempted to tell it we were safe, but it didn't listen. Everette gave my back a supportive rub. "Hey, Shelby, look at me. He's upset with me, not you. And he's not even that upset. That's pretty much how he sounds when he's happy too."

Bradford's expression softened and his lips pressed in an almost apologetic line. "On my worst day, in my worst mood, no woman would ever have anything to fear from me. My wife says I'm a desert cactus, all prickly and ugly on the outside, and gooey on the inside."

"Joanna says that?" Everette asked.

Bradford's eyes narrowed. "I'm trying to make Shelby feel better."

"Gooey? Are you sure that's the word she used? I bet she called you a softie and you fixated on the cactus part and are remembering that wrong."

Bradford folded his arms across his wide chest and sighed.

It might have been the lack of fear in Everette as he joked with Bradford, but I began to relax. "You're not ugly," I said softly. Bradford wasn't. The marks on his face were intimidating rather than disfiguring.

He smiled. "Doesn't matter if I am. I go home every night to the love of my life. As long as this face works for her, I don't care what the rest of the world thinks of it."

Awww. I lowered the bat and placed it against the wall. "Would you like to come in?"

Everette surprised me by not seeming keen on that. "He's probably too busy to do more than just say hello."

What was I missing? I met Bradford's gaze. "Did you just come by to say hello?" That was sweet, but something told me gooey or not, there was another reason he was there.

"Actually," Bradford said, "there's a job I'm having difficulty with."

My eyes rounded. "A case? Like finding a missing child?"

"Something like that. Normally I don't take on this kind of work, but it's a favor for a good friend of mine."

"And you came to Everette for help?"

Bradford nodded.

The side glance I shot Everette was full of wonder. "This

is what you've talked about. I could see it firsthand." I frowned and returned my attention to Bradford. "Unless it's top secret, then I'll understand. I've been training, but I understand that there are things I can't know until I've passed the testing phase."

Bradford cocked an eyebrow at Everette. "It's a complicated process. Some might say unnecessarily so, but you're correct, there are things you won't be informed of at this time. We could, however, use your assistance if you're okay not knowing the full details."

Was I?

Could I charge blindly ahead?

What was the alternative? Staying as I was? Going backward? No, neither of those options were acceptable. And what if . . . what if taking on this job helped me gain even more confidence? My goal needed to be to not freak out and grab a baseball bat when someone knocked on my door. So far, Everette was doing more to help me reach that goal than I'd thought anyone could. "Yes. I'd love to help in any way I can."

"Good," Bradford said. "Then the information regarding the job will be sent to your phone, Everette. Disseminate it as you feel is appropriate. I'll be doing my part to ensure this goes smoothly."

Everette shook Bradford's hand. "Thanks. Sorry I seemed reluctant at first. I'd started to imagine this week going in a different direction."

Shaking his head, Bradford said, "If you decide to not do this, text me. I'm not saying I'd be happy about it, but I'd get over it."

"No," Everette said, "I appreciate everything you've done. This is a go."

"Okay," Bradford said before turning his attention back to me. A shadow darkened his face. "A long time ago I lost my sister because some soulless men thought they could do whatever they wanted to. The experience left me with scars on the inside as well. We all have our demons and we wouldn't be human if they didn't sometimes win. But it gets better, especially if you surround yourself with good people."

I wiped away the tears that brought to my eyes. Yes, this man understood. "Thank you."

Bradford nodded at Everette. "People don't come any better than the man you've got beside you right now."

"Did you just say something nice about me?" Everette joked, bringing a hand to his chest in shock.

Bradford rolled his eyes. "I didn't say he wasn't a pain in the ass, but it's impossible to stay upset with him. Not when he looks at you with those sad, puppy-dog eyes."

"Puppy-dog? Really?" Everette began to close the door in Bradford's face. "Looks like your time here is done. Bye."

"Nice to meet you." I leaned forward and waved at Bradford before the door closed. He smiled and waved back. "So, that's Bradford."

"Yep."

I brought both hands to my face in excitement. "Am I really going to help you find someone?"

Everette looked away then back at me. "I'll need to look over the job before I can agree to that, but if it sounds safe, then yes."

Clasping my hands in front of me, I squealed, "I can't believe this is happening. I mean, really happening. Is it okay if I tell Megan about it?"

"Can you trust her to keep it to herself?"

"Absolutely."

"Then yes."

"This is so exciting."

"I would have preferred if the timing of it was next week, but if you're happy, I'm happy."

I grinned. "I'm thrilled. Since meeting you, every day has given me something wonderful to look forward to. I don't know what this job entails, but I am ready for the challenge."

He tucked a lock of my hair behind my ear. "That's exactly how I hoped you'd feel."

It was an odd thing to say, but I told myself it made sense in terms of everything we'd done that week. He'd told me he'd help me increase my confidence and, for the most part, he was doing that.

The fear from earlier had fallen away and knowing that I was entrusted with an important search for someone had me feeling—heroic. "Hey," I said breathlessly, "want to go for a run?"

"A run?" He laughed, shook his head as if freeing himself of a different thought, and said, "I would love that."

Chapter Eighteen

Shelby

WHILE WAITING FOR the information to come in, Everette and I went for a short run. There was an intimacy to that shared time together that was almost as good as an after-sex snuggle. He wasn't as lean as most runners were, so he got winded quicker than I did, but if we kept an even pace we were able to talk and laugh as we went.

Had we been sitting somewhere when he asked me about my parents, I wouldn't have been able to hold back the sadness. There was a feeling of freedom, though, that came with each pump of my arms and legs. I hadn't died along with them. I was still very much alive and that was how I decided my good memories of my parents needed to be.

I told Everette about the time my dad had taken me fishing because he'd heard a song about a father and daughter bonding "just fishing." Neither of us had wanted to bait the hook. He'd been as bad at casting the line as I was. The poor fish we'd caught had endured both of us trying to figure out what to do with it before we struggled to remove the hook and set it free. I was ten or so years old. What I remember most about that day was how long we both sat there looking out at the water after releasing the fish. Eventually, without turning toward me, he'd said, "I've never fished before."

With a heart full of love for him, I'd said, "Really? You're a natural."

We'd both burst out laughing and did so until we were wiping tears from our eyes. Eventually, he'd said, "Next time let's go to a museum and then for sushi. That's the only kind of fish I like."

"Deal."

Neither of my parents had been the outdoorsy type. My mother's idea of a perfect day was nothing scheduled and all of us engrossed in a book we'd call our favorite until we fell in love with our next read. She loved to explore the world but only through the books she read. She used to say she knew my father was the man for her when his excuse for why he was late to pick her up for a date was that he'd only had one chapter left and couldn't leave the story before he knew how it ended.

I had so many memories of them, cuddled side by side on the couch, each with their own book and a pen. They'd write little notes in the margins as they read and then switch books. The magic happened when they read the other's book along with their annotations. Every once in a while, they'd stop to exchange a smile or hug. I didn't know how rare their bond was until I started dating and realized how difficult it could be to make any connection with a person at all.

I enjoyed reading, but not like my parents. The same kind of peace my parents had found in the pages of a fresh story, I found in nature and moving through it.

When I glanced at Everette he smiled at me and it felt like no one else was in the world beyond the two of us. Was this what my parents had—this connection? I didn't share that pondering with Everette. It felt like too much, too early, but it was becoming difficult to imagine my life without Everette in it.

We followed the run with a shared shower, a leisurely exploration of each other, and a nap. Hunger drove us finally to dress and head down to the kitchen to forage. I loved that Everette didn't expect me to cook for him. We tossed around options for what to make, decided on baked chicken and a salad, and each chose a part of it to prepare. His mother had raised him well.

We were seated across from each other at the dining room table, finishing up our late lunch, when his phone buzzed with a message. I couldn't contain my excitement. "Is it from Bradford?"

He checked his messages. "It is."

"About the job?"

Nodding, he raised a finger in a request for me to give him a moment as he read what Bradford had sent. "This does sound like something you could help with."

I nearly bounced out of my seat. "Seriously?"

"I can't give you all the information, but yes."

Tapping my fingers on the table in anticipation, I gushed, "I completely understand that I'm not yet part of whatever organization you work for, but I promise I'll make a valuable contribution. I've always been good with details and problem-solving. I'm also good with keeping what's confidential to myself."

He took a moment to read over something on his phone, then said, "Before I tell you anything, I need to explain something. The people I work with are only able to do what they do because they fly under the radar. We use aliases, burner phones, rental cars, and clothing designed to make our faces indistinguishable to surveillance cameras. Very rarely do things go as planned. It's not unusual to bend or break laws while bringing home an innocent. That can not only be disconcerting, but it also can put anyone affiliated with this process in potential legal trouble."

"So working with you could land me in jail?"

He replaced his phone in his pocket. "We're not without resources. I'd like to think it would never come to that, but the risk is there—yes."

That was something I hadn't considered. The whole scenario took me a moment to soak in. "So, if I work with you on this job, I have to leave my phone behind and not tell anyone where I'm going?" I didn't know if I could do that.

He rubbed a hand over his chin. "When put that way, it sounds worse than it is. Those in the organization have a level of trust that makes it easy for us to agree to those terms. Since you're not yet one of us and you won't have access to sensitive intel—I'd say it would be fine for you to tell one person about this."

"Megan?"

"If she's your person."

I searched his face. Part of me wanted to say it wasn't

necessary, but the blind trust I had in humanity had been shattered. "I could call her now and she could hear all of this?"

"Do you trust her?"

"With my life."

"Then yes."

I took out my phone and called her. "Megan? Do you have a minute?"

"Sure. I was about to take a break. What's up?"

I cleared my throat. "Everette has been asked to help find someone." Everette nodded in confirmation. "And he's allowing me to assist on a limited basis."

Megan's tone turned cautious. "That's—interesting."

"It'll mean going off the grid so our involvement will be a secret."

"I don't like any part of this," she said.

I'd been afraid of that. I was torn between needing a voice of reason and resenting that she couldn't also be excited about this opportunity. "He's here with me. I'd like to put you on speakerphone so you can hear it as he tells me about it."

"Okay."

"You're welcome to put me on video as well," Everette said. "Take some snapshots if you'd like. I understand why you wouldn't trust me. You don't know me yet."

I switched over to video and turned the camera's direction so Everette's face filled the screen. "Everette, this is my best friend, Megan. Megan, this is Everette."

Everette smiled and waved.

Megan's smile was a little forced, but she waved back.

"Okay, Everette," I said, "tell us about this job."

Without missing a beat, Everette dove in. "Normally, the people we seek are minors who've been taken by someone, but this request is less . . . urgent. A friend of a friend recently went MIA after visiting a town about twenty minutes south of here. She's been talking about wanting to get away and start over. There's no reason to believe she's in any danger, but there has been no contact from her. It's been requested that we find her and assess if she's happily taking time away or if she's in need of assistance."

It didn't seem difficult to locate an adult in the modern age of everything digital. "Have there been charges to her credit card? Can't someone track her phone?"

"She has her phone turned off, and if she's buying anything, it must be in cash."

"Hold on," Megan said. "Is this friend of a friend married?"

"Yes."

"How do we know she's not hiding for a reason and that finding her wouldn't be what puts her at risk?"

Megan's question was valid. I met Everette's gaze.

Everette hesitated for a breath, then said, "There's some amount of trust required for taking any of these jobs. I can't say with one hundred percent certainty that this woman wants to be found, but what I can promise is that if she doesn't want her location disclosed, we won't report it to anyone. All I've been asked to do is confirm that she's safe."

Megan shook her head. "And whoever paid you would

be okay with that? I don't think so."

"Respectfully," Everette answered, "it doesn't matter what you think—this is what we do. The people who hire us know we don't follow the rules . . . not theirs, not the government's. Although I am a man of humble means, there are some powerful players in the organization I work for. If I report that this woman is better off left alone or under their protection, she'll have the resources she needs to ensure her safety."

"Do you work for the Mafia or something?" Megan asked.

"No." Everette sighed. "The way it was explained to me was to imagine a coin with two sides. On one side, there are powerful people using their wealth and influence for their own gain. On the other side, there are other, equally powerful people who keep them in check. When it comes to helping someone in need, I never have to ask if we can afford to do what needs to be done. What I ask myself is how I can do it in a way that doesn't give the other side the power to shut us down."

"Are you sure you're on the good side?" I asked in a near whisper.

His gaze was unguarded when he said, "I know I am. Children come home because of what these people do. Battered women land in safer places. I've personally handed a baby back to sobbing parents who thought they'd never see their child again after it was snatched from a playground. So, although there are many things I don't know, I don't question if I'm on the right side."

Megan's lips pursed, then she asked, "What's this woman's name?"

"That's not information I'm at liberty to share."

"What can you tell us?" I asked.

Everette looked away then back at me. "I can give you her physical description. She's about your height, dark hair, late twenties. She took her dog with her when she left. He's a young black Labrador retriever. We have the last town she was in before she turned off her phone and a strong lead that she's still in that area."

"Does she have family nearby?" I asked.

"That's where I'd start," Megan added.

Everette shook his head. "None that are known. Also, there's no record of her owning property there."

I chewed my bottom lip. "She'd have to stay somewhere that allows dogs. That at least limits the places we'd look."

"That's good thinking." Everette smiled.

"You might want to check out the dog parks," Megan said. "People tend to frequent the same ones. Someone might have seen her."

"Another good idea."

"She'll have to buy dog food. We could ask about her at the local pet stores," I suggested.

"I like it. I'll need to pick up a few supplies, but we could begin this search in an hour or so when I return."

I flipped the phone camera back so I could see Megan's face. "I want to do this. What do you think?"

She let out a slow, audible breath before answering. "It doesn't sound dangerous, but call me every day. I'll tell work there's a pending family emergency so if you need me, I can be there quickly."

Lowering my voice even though Everette was right there and able to hear me, I said, "I realize this sounds implausible and often what doesn't sound true isn't, but I trust Everette. If he says this is about making sure a woman is safe and ensuring she remains that way—I believe him."

Everette frowned, then cleared his throat.

Megan didn't respond immediately. She seemed to be weighing her next words. Finally, she said, "You look happier than I've seen you in a long time. Everette, can you hear me?"

"Yes," he answered.

"I know what you look like and I'm also good at tracking people down. If you hurt Shelby, run and hide, but don't get too comfortable because when I find you—and I will find you—I'll make your testicles into a snack for my pet turtle."

"Okay, that's oddly specific." He cleared his throat again. "Thankfully I can confidently say I would never hurt Shelby."

"So that's good," I joked. "Yay, for safe testicles."

Neither of them laughed. Although I understood why, after nearly half a year of feeling heavy with grief, I wanted to embrace the thrill of this search. "Everette, you said you use aliases. Do you have one for us?"

He nodded. "It would make sense if we're a dog-owning couple considering moving to the area. That would give us a conversation starter with people at dog parks as well as pet stores."

I couldn't contain the smile that spread across my face. "We're going undercover."

He smiled back. "Yes, we are."

Megan didn't say anything, but there was still worry in her expression. "Every day, that's when you need to call me. Every single day."

"I will," I promised.

Chapter Nineteen

Everette

A FEW HOURS later, I parked my rental car in a lot beside the second dog park we'd put on our list to canvas that day. Shelby liked making lists, which helped when it came to making sure the people Bradford planted would be at the right place at the right time. To be believable, the search couldn't be made too easy, so although we'd each spoken to several people at the last dog park, no one had seen a young woman with a black Labrador.

I'll admit it was amusing to see Clay Landon standing in the park holding his small light brown dog, Boppy. Since coming to Driverton, Clay had started dressing more casually so he didn't look as awkward as he once had in jeans and an oxford. There was still a certain polish to him that implied wealth, but at least he was learning to tone it down.

After unbuckling my seat belt, I turned to Shelby. "You did well at that last park. Do the same thing here. Remember we're just two people scoping out the place, asking if this is the park our friend recommended. You've been working in the description of her perfectly. The goal is to be friendly, get the information we need, and to leave without being re-membered. Give them nothing interesting to repeat about us that doesn't fit the narrative."

She nodded vigorously. "I've got this. At first it felt weird to lie to people. I don't do that generally. But I just keep telling myself this is for a good cause and I'm feeling okay with it."

That was essentially what I was doing each time I lied to her. Normally, I considered honesty the foundation of a relationship, but she looked so fucking happy on this quest. Some lies, just like some sins, had to be okay.

"I have a good feeling about this park," I said just before I leaned over and gave her a quick kiss.

Her smile warmed me from head to toe. "Me too."

A heartbeat later, we were in the park speaking to an old-er woman who owned a pug. She hadn't seen the woman we said was our friend, but we did get to hear the story of her gallbladder attack that ended up just being gas. We didn't escape from her orbit before learning the names of all of her children, some of her grandchildren, and about her hus-band's recent non-cancerous mole removal.

Shelby and I were both smiling when the woman paused to ask her pug if he was thirsty and we used that as an opportunity to bolt. The next woman we spoke to was visibly annoyed that she had to put her Kindle down to speak to us. She also hadn't seen a black Labrador at the park, but my guess was that she never saw much, considering how quickly she ended the conversation with us and re-turned to reading.

"Third one is the charm," Shelby said with optimism as she nodded toward Clay.

"Here's hoping." I did my best to sound less than hopeful.

"Excuse me," Shelby said as we came within a few feet of Clay. "My boyfriend and I are moving to this area with our dog. Our friend suggested a dog park and we're not sure if this is the one she was referring to."

"Could be. There are a few around. Although this is my favorite."

My jaw went slack at how normal Clay sounded. Friendly but reserved. Absolutely believable.

Shelby slipped an arm through mine. "Look, hon, he has a Havanese. That's one of my favorite breeds."

Clay's face lit up. "Her name is Boppy."

"She's gorgeous," Shelby cooed. "Aren't you, little one? Her coloring is spectacular. And her grooming is perfection. Do you have her done locally?"

"I'm new to the area," Clay said. "But my wife will beam when I tell her what you said. She prides herself on taking Boppy to only the best."

"Well, I can see why," Shelby said with a warm smile. "Have you had her long? Boppy, not your wife."

She's good. It didn't take her long to figure out that everyone's favorite subject was themselves and that humor was an excellent icebreaker.

Clay talked about how he and his wife had bought Boppy soon after they'd married and how much joy she'd brought them. His expression darkened slightly when he said they'd been trying to have a child for years, but so far, they'd been unsuccessful.

Shelby's compassion for him was touching. "I'll send up a prayer for your family. Things don't always turn out the way we hope they will, but it sounds like you have a lot of love to give a child."

The emotion that shone in Clay's eyes took me by surprise. I had no idea he and his wife had struggled to conceive. Until then, I'd only seen Clay as Cooper's rich older brother. I'd just assumed that anyone with his amount of money didn't have problems. Considering what had gone down with their uncle, I should have known better.

"Thank you," Clay said in a husky tone, then added, "So what did your friend tell you about the park she loves?"

Shelby exchanged a look with me that I wasn't sure how to interpret. "Not much, but maybe you've seen her. She has a black Lab. He's young. About a year or so old."

Clay nodded. "I have seen a woman with a black Lab. Accessorized impressively. From his collar and leash to his bowl and toys. You can tell she spoils him, but not with things from a department store. I usually keep to myself at parks, but next time I see her I'll have to ask her which pet store she shops at because my wife loves to match Boppy's outfits to hers."

"I bet she'd love that. When I talk to her later today I'll pass along your compliment. I'm sure that'll make her day." With that, Shelby looked across to where a woman was sitting on the ground playing with a puppy. "It's been wonderful talking to you. Do you think that woman would mind if I say hello to her pup?" Shelby walked away without waiting for Clay to respond. Her enthusiasm about meeting the puppy seemed genuine.

In a low voice, I said, "Thanks Clay. I really appreciate this."

With a bland expression, Clay cuddled his dog to one side of his face. "If this game of yours fails, I don't want to brag, but I'm an expert matchmaker. I could fly the two of you off to Europe on a trip so romantic you'd be married before returning home."

Without taking my eyes off Shelby who was bent over petting the puppy, I said, "I appreciate that, but I've got this under control."

"If you've never spent a month on a yacht touring the Mediterranean, that's also incredibly romantic."

"What you've done today was enough."

Clay grunted. "I don't understand Driverton. Why are you all too damn proud to accept help?"

"We aren't. Not when it comes from one of us." That had come out harsher than I'd meant for it to. "What I mean is—"

"No, I understand and this is nothing new to me. I can bend over backward to help people, support them, cheer them on, but somehow, I always end up on the outside looking in. It was like that with my family. It's been like that with the Barringtons. Lexi is the only one who makes me feel valued for who I am."

"I'm sorry to hear that." I was. It sounded like a lonely existence and not at all how I'd grown up feeling.

"Like this thing you're doing in Driverton. This 'organization' Bradford and Cooper are creating. No one asked me if I'd like to be part of it."

"Did you want to be?"

"It'd be nice to be fucking asked."

My eyebrows shot up. "I'm not in a place where I can make any of those decisions, but I can mention it to Bradford."

"Don't bother," Clay said. "I know what he thinks of me, and it's no different than what you probably do. You think I haven't known struggle because I've never known poverty."

"I wouldn't say that."

"But you don't know what a person has been through if you've never walked in their shoes."

"I agree." *How do I extricate myself from this conversation before Clay gives away that he knows me?*

"I like you."

This is going down an uncomfortable path fast. "Thank you."

"And despite what you think, I'm a force to be reckoned with."

"I'm sure you are."

"Essentially I do what I want when I want."

"Good?" I took out my phone, preparing to pretend I'd received a call.

He cleared his throat. "It's important to me that you and the people in Driverton know how much it means to me that you took in Cooper when he was on the run from our uncle. All of you accepted him, protected him, made sure he never felt alone. I owe you more than I could ever repay. And that's why I won't take no for an answer."

"Excuse me?"

"I paid off your parents' mortgage. Everyone's in town, actually. Just because you don't think I could keep quiet about the 'jobs' you're taking on, doesn't mean I can't also be a hero."

My mouth dropped open. "What the fuck did you do?"

"You heard me."

"You're serious."

"And I did it in a sneaky way that makes it look like reparations came in from an old government land grab for a logging company that tore this area up about a hundred years ago. Which means no one but you will know it was me. See, not only can I do good things, but I can keep my mouth shut about it."

My head was spinning with what he'd done and what that would mean to my friends and family. They would never have accepted the money from him, but if they thought it was due to them—yes, they would and they'd feel good about it. "You didn't have to do that, Clay."

His jaw tightened. "I know I'm not *one of you* but I can't begin to repay how grateful I am to all of you for taking my family in. That's all this is."

It didn't feel real or like something that could happen. On the other hand, Clay was one of the wealthiest men in the world. He'd probably spent more on his shoes than the mortgages, but it was still incredibly, unfathomably generous. "Next time I'm hanging out at Little Willie's, I'll call you. Levi and Ollie are not in a great place—even if you cleared their biggest bills. I want to help them, but I'm not sure if I know how. It's time for them to stop drinking and start working toward those goals they've given up as out of reach. Levi makes the best moonshine north of the Carolinas. Bradford found him contacts who could help him make an income from it, but he hasn't followed through. Ollie is one of the most generous people I know, but he self-sabotages too. I was right there with them until recently, drinking away my potential. I understand how comfortable giving up is—but they are capable of so much more." I told him what they'd done on day one of Bradford's boot camp. "Maybe I'm wrong. Maybe I should let them live their lives any way they want to, but it's hard to move on and not take them with me."

"I don't drink moonshine," Clay said in a serious tone.

I exchanged a look with him and laughed. His humor was so dry I was sure many missed it. When the mood sobered, I said, "I'm sorry you've struggled to find where you fit in, Clay. Driverton is full of people who've been there and felt that. You want to be one of us? I'll show you how. Mostly, it's about showing up, not showing off, and taking care of each other. If you ever feel like you need some self-correcting, spend a little time with Mrs. Williams. She'll cut your ego right down and set you back on a humble course."

He smiled. "She scares me a little."

I nodded. "See, you already think like us." When Shelby sought my gaze, I said, "I have to go. Thanks again for today. And for what you did for the town. You're one crazy son of a bitch, but if you can put up with us I guess we can put up with you. Don't be a stranger."

Chapter Twenty

Shelby

B ACK AT THE house, I curled up on one corner of a couch with my cell phone. My mind was racing with ideas for where the woman we were searching for might be. Using an app, I charted out the route we'd take the next day—starting with the closest stores then to boutique shops a little farther out.

Everette came to sit beside me. I shifted my weight to snuggle against him rather than the arm of the couch, and he wrapped an arm around my back. "What are you doing?"

I turned my phone toward him. "These are the places I think we should hit tomorrow. I'm figuring out which order would allow us to go to the most in the least amount of time."

He kissed the top of my head. "Wow. That's impressive."

I glanced up at him through my lashes. "I like to organize things. I always have. I miss that about my old job. Putting in orders and tracking stock doesn't sound exciting to some, but I get a little giddy whenever I find trends and can predict a shortage. Computer programs can do some of that faster, but my success has also come from trusting my intuition. Numbers can lie or at least mislead. I know AI is advancing fast, but the human element is something I don't believe it will ever be able to recreate."

"I hope you're right."

"Take what we're wearing for example. I would never have thought a shirt could fool a camera into not seeing my face. How cool is that?"

"It is awesome."

"But without us in it, what would it be?" I stretched up and gave him a deep kiss full of all the gratitude welling within me. He claimed my mouth hungrily as he gathered me closer, pulling me onto his lap and the prominent evidence that he wanted me. I gave myself over to the passion that flared between us. There was no holding back when it came to him—no need to.

The shirt I'd considered incredible a moment before quickly became an unnecessary barrier between us. Kissing wildly, we whipped our shirts off, then shifted and shimmied until we were skin to skin. I straddled him, moving my sex up and down along the length of his shaft.

His hands teased and worshipped my breasts, bringing each one to his mouth in turn. I arched into the pleasure, gripping his shoulders for balance. I tasted his neck, nibbling my way up to the lobe of his ear. He brought a hand between us and expertly, rhythmically circled my clit until I was jutting against his hand.

As my excitement grew, so did my impatience. I dragged

his mouth back to mine, fucking his mouth with my tongue as forcefully as I wanted to be taken. It was a clear signal he interpreted correctly. Bringing his hands to my hips, he guided his tip to my center then thrust upward into me.

All those big muscles of his, the ones that didn't work in his favor when we were running, were gloriously powerful when it came to sex. I rode him from above, but he met me thrust for powerful thrust. With him, I could abandon all worry of falling or hurting him. I let myself go, clung to him as he stood, and cried out his name when he bent me backward over the couch, supporting me only with one hand behind my back and pounded into me.

So strong.

So in control.

I was his in a way I never thought I could belong to a man.

Just before I came, he dragged me up so he could kiss me again then joined me with a series of hard and fast thrusts that were nearly too much for me in the most mind-blowing way. Each time with him was better than the last, but this time my orgasm rode in on an emotional high that brought me as close to heaven as a living person can go.

I collapsed against his strong chest. He slid out of me then gathered me to him and gave me the kind of hug only a lover who has also become your best friend gives. I buried my face in his neck and smiled.

"Do you think we could both fit in your bathtub?" he asked.

I chuckled as I imagined his large frame filling it and the

contortionist moves I'd have to perform to join him. Would there even be room for water? Did it matter? "Let's try it." It was an oversized tub that would have worked for a normal couple, but Everette was not only tall, he was beefy as well. I linked my legs around his waist as he walked across the living room and up the stairs to my bedroom.

There was something incredibly hot about how little effort it took him to carry me around. He was able to close the tub drain and turn on the water without putting me down. Finally, when the water was halfway up, he placed me back on my feet and gingerly tested it with his toes. I'm not sure I've ever seen anything more adorable. After shooting me a smile and a thumbs-up, he climbed in and sat down. It was tight, but with his legs bent, he fit. The water stopped just below the overflow drain. "Come on in," he invited.

I took a moment to assess how to best do that, then stepped in and sat between his legs. He shifted me back until his half-erect cock nestled against my lower back. With encouragement from him, I relaxed more until the back of my head was supported by his chest.

He reached for a washcloth and soap. I closed my eyes and sighed as he began to wash me. Never had I felt so adored. The warm slipperiness of his soap-covered hand was followed by a rinse of water he squeezed from the washcloth.

Between shoulder and neck kisses, he soaped my breasts, arms, legs, then lifted me to wash me intimately. I bit my lip and spread my legs as wide as I could in the confines of the tub. When he lowered me back into the water, his hand stayed on my sex and those gifted fingers of his dipped inside me.

I gripped his knees while he stroked me, plunged in and out of me, and brought me to climax yet again. This time, rather than holding me to him, he lifted me so I was on my knees before him and drove his tongue deep within me. I was done, but he was far from it. He licked me intimately from front to back then the water sloshed as he changed position to stand in the tub. I stood as well and bent over, holding the edge of the tub.

"You're so fucking perfect," he growled from behind, giving one of my butt cheeks a slap that stung. That was all it took for my body to decide it was ready for another round. With one hand he grabbed my hair, pulling back until I was arching my ass higher for him.

"Less talking, more fucking," I purred.

He didn't need to be told twice. With one arm wrapped around me to steady me, he slammed into me from behind, relentlessly, savagely. I moved to welcome him deeper, sobbing for him to not stop, to take me harder, deeper. Wave after wave of pleasure rolled through me as he did just that and gave me an orgasm so good I knew I'd still be smiling about it years later. He was in no rush to join me, prolonging my pleasure. His release came with a swear, a grunt, and a final thrust that left me feeling shattered and finally whole again at the same time.

After withdrawing, he sat back in the water. My legs were shaking, but with assistance, I returned to my place against him again. "I wasn't a bath person," he murmured against my hair, "but I may have just changed my mind."

"Me too," I whispered, incapable of forming or articulating more of a response than that. My mind was blissfully devoid of thought of anything beyond how good I felt and how good he felt against me.

He turned on the faucet, surrounding us again with warm water. I expressed my pleasure with a happy groan and snuggled closer to him. "I've also never felt so territorial about a woman," he murmured against my hair. "I want all of this, all of you, today, tomorrow and . . ."

He didn't say forever and maybe it would have been too much if he had, but I understood how he felt. Whatever this was, it was more intense than anything I'd ever been a part of. He'd asked me to say I was his and I had, but often words voiced in moments of passion were just that. This wasn't like that. I belonged to him, with him. He belonged to me, with me. I believed that to my core.

And rather than it being scary, it felt like a miracle I hadn't dared hope could happen. "I feel the same," I said breathlessly.

"Good, because this is just the beginning for us."

Chapter Twenty-One

Everette

WHEN PEOPLE TALKED about falling in love, they often described it as gut-wrenching and scary. That wasn't at all how it felt with Shelby. She and I clicked together easily, like the final piece of a puzzle. I'd never been one to believe in fate, but she and I felt like we were meant to be.

I was thinking about that the next day as we walked into a dog clothing boutique that had been third on Shelby's list. Despite how neither of the first two shops had produced any leads, Shelby was glowing and the smiles she kept shooting my way made me glad we were at the store where Clay's wife, Lexi, would be.

One hand laced with mine, Shelby dragged me from aisle to aisle, exclaiming how adorable the merchandise was. It might have been, but all I had eyes for was her. We were stepping away from dresses I was certain no dog needed when Lexi appeared at the register and greeted us.

"Welcome," she said. "If you have any questions or would like anything in a size you don't see, please don't feel shy about asking."

"This store is amazing," Shelby gushed. "Are the products handmade?"

Lexi proved to be as good an actor as Clay when she beamed with pride. "Yes, they are. I make all of the collections myself. It started as a passion for my own pup then just sort of grew."

"Really? I love that. What kind of dog do you have?"

"A Havanese," Lexi said and Shelby looked at me in surprise.

"What a great breed. We met someone yesterday with one. Maybe you know him. I didn't get the man's name, but the dog was Boppy."

Lexi's eyebrows rose. "Oh, yes. I've seen that dog around. She's beautiful."

The sound of a dog whining from a back room caught Shelby's attention. "Is that yours I hear?"

I pinned Lexi with a look and shook my head.

With a smooth smile, Lexi said, "Oh, no, I'm boarding a dog for a friend. I'd let her out in the store, but she's so shy it would traumatize her."

Shelby nodded. "That's sad, but understandable. We left our dog at home for the same reason. Our goal is to socialize him more, but we wanted to scope out this area without him."

"Scope it out?" Lexi feigned interest in our cover story. "Are you new to the area?"

Moving closer, to hug my arm to her side, Shelby said, "Not yet, but we hope to be. We have a friend who lives a short bit away from here and she says this is a very dog-friendly town. I wonder if she's been here. She's about my age with a black Labrador. She just recently moved to the area."

"I think I have met her. Very nice woman. She picked up a collar and leash to match her outfit."

"That sounds like her."

Okay, so things were getting back on track. I began to relax.

Lexi looked around as if she was remembering something. "She was asking me about things to do with her dog and I suggested a fundraiser the local shelter is having tomorrow. I gave her a flyer; I think I have an extra one. Hang on."

"Oh, that would be wonderful," Shelby said.

Lexi bent to look on some shelves, then whipped out a paper and handed it to Shelby. "There should be a good turnout. It might be fun for you as well if you'd like to meet other dog owners in the area. Some of them get together for playdates and such."

After reading over the flyer, Shelby showed it to me. "This. This is exactly what we've been looking for."

I hugged her to my side, so happy to see her not only smiling but confident and proud of herself. "It is."

"Thank you," Shelby said to Lexi. "Will you be at the fundraiser tomorrow?"

Lexi looked stumped by the question before she said, "I may be."

"Thank you for everything. If we move to this area, I'm sure we'll see you again," Shelby said before she and I made our way out of the store to our car.

After Shelby gave me directions to the next store on her list, she said, "What a nice woman." Shelby said it with such sincerity I imagined the two of them becoming friends.

"I agree. Hey, are you tired? If so, we can head back. That fundraiser sounds like a solid lead."

A smile spread across Shelby's face. "It does, doesn't it? We're so close to finding her. I can feel it. Still, there's only three more stores on my list. Who knows, we might meet someone else who's seen her."

"Right." That wasn't possible, but I couldn't say it. Her obvious enjoyment of the search had me turning onto the road in the direction of the next store. "Before we're done, we'll know every dog owner in this area."

"That's how it's done, right? You leave no stone un-turned."

She was right. "That's how it's done."

Her hand closed on my thigh. "Thank you for letting me be a part of this, Everette. It means so much that you trust me."

I covered her hand with mine. "Of course."

"Trust has been something I've struggled with since los-ing my parents. I wasn't sure I'd ever get past that, but you've become my calm harbor from the storm of life. I feel safe with you, safer than I ever thought I would again."

I frowned with a prick of worry that the next day wouldn't go as well as I planned. *No, it will. I've thought of everything.* We were even scheduled to have dinner with Clay, Lexi, Bradford, and Joanna. I smiled as I imagined how we could now all laugh over how having Boppy at the boutique had almost ended the game a day early. "I'm honored to be that for you. What you went through—no one should ever endure something like that—but you're not alone anymore. You've got your own personal hero, and I'm not going anywhere."

Chapter Twenty-Two

Shelby

THE NEXT DAY, after sleeping in instead of going for a run, Everette and I headed off to the fundraiser. I was so freaking excited, I FaceTimed Megan on the way. "This is it," I said when she answered. "I have a really strong feeling this is the day we'll find her."

"I do too," Everette said with a smile.

Sounding almost as giddy as I felt, Megan said, "I wish I could be there with you. I'm so invested in how this turns out. What do you plan to say to her when you see her?"

I glanced at Everette's profile. "I think we should be honest about why we're there and make it known right from the start that if she doesn't want anyone to know where she is, her secret will be safe with us."

"I wonder how she'll take that," Megan said.

Everette met my gaze quickly before returning his attention to the road. "I'm sure it'll work out even better than we expect it to."

Smiling at the woman who was family in my heart, I gurgled, "Megan, look at me; I've found something to get out of bed for. I can't tell you how good this feels. If you'd told me a month ago I'd be tracking down lost people with this incredible man, I wouldn't have believed it."

"Incredible, huh?" Everette parroted with a grin.

I laughed while rolling my eyes. "Keep that ego in check, buddy, or you won't be able to squeeze that big head of yours out your car door."

"That's it," Megan joked, "keep him humble." After a moment, in a more serious tone, she added, "Everette, this is exactly what Shelby needed. I've got my best friend back. Thank you."

"You're welcome," Everette said easily. "After this case, let's all get together. I'd love for Shelby's people to meet mine."

"I am your people, Shelby." Megan pointed at her heart then to me. "Always have been, always will be." To Everette, she joked, "Are any of your people as hot as you are? If so, I'm packing now."

He laughed off that comment. I did as well and ended the call because we'd arrived at the animal shelter. Rather than immediately opening the door, I took a deep breath and soaked the moment in. "I don't want to be disappointed if she's not there, but I really believe she will be."

"I do too." Everette cupped a hand under my chin and turned my face toward his. The kiss he gave me warmed me to my toes. "Do you know how much you mean to me?"

When he raised his head, I lost myself in the beauty and intensity of his gaze. "Hopefully as much as you mean to me."

It might have been a moment or an eternity that we sat there simply staring into each other's eyes before he released my chin and said, "Okay, let's go find this woman."

"Yes."

Yes to that idea.

Yes to everything when it came to him.

Several vendors had pop-up tents set up on the lawn in front of the building. People with dogs were walking from one area to the next. I looked around as we walked but didn't see a woman with a black Labrador.

"She'll be here," Everette promised.

I nodded, holding to my belief that she would. The grassy area along one side of the shelter also had a line of vendors. We headed that way. It was only when we rounded the corner of the building that I saw her.

There, sitting on a picnic blanket, was a woman about my age with a black Labrador sporting a collar and leash that matched her dress. "That's her," I whispered urgently.

"I bet you're right."

A thought came to me that had me gripping Everette's hand tightly. "Give me a moment to talk to her alone. You're . . . huge and that can be intimidating. I'll talk to her for a moment, gain her trust, and explain who we are. If she's afraid of her husband, I think she'd be more comfortable telling a woman." Everette opened his mouth and looked about to shoot down my suggestion, but I placed my hand gently on his lips and said, "Please. Trust me." I lowered my hand and waited.

He grimaced, then said, "She doesn't look afraid to me.

It's not that I don't trust you, it's just that—"

"You don't think I can do this?" That hurt.

"No. That's not it at all." He sighed. "It's just not how I thought this would go."

Grasping for what that could mean, I asked, "Are you worried about not getting credit for the find? I don't care what you tell people. I just know that, as a woman, it's easier to be honest about some things with women than men."

He rubbed a hand over his face and squared his shoulders. "Okay. I wanted to be right there with you, but I guess it doesn't matter. I'll watch from here."

I touched his cheek and looked into his eyes. "You don't have to worry about me. I'll be just a few feet away."

He nodded. "You're right. Go. I'll be right here."

With one last fortifying deep breath, I turned on my heel and walked over to where the woman was rising to her feet. "Excuse me," I said.

A huge smile spread across her face. "You found me."

It was not at all the reaction I'd expected. Did she think I was someone else? "My name is Shelby. Do you mind if I ask a question?"

"Hi, Shelby. Not at all." With her free hand she gave the dog at her side a pat. "This is Tyr. You can change his name if you'd like, but he responds to it so I think he likes it."

"I'm sorry?"

"You don't know about him? Oh, I guess you couldn't because that would have given everything away." She held out the leash to me. "It's never a good idea to spring a dog on someone as a gift, but I understand why Everette would think having one would be good for you."

Not accepting the leash, I looked back at Everette in confusion. "You know Everette?"

Her voice deepened with concern. "Am I doing this wrong? I wasn't given a story to tell you. All I'm supposed to do is meet you and Everette here with Tyr."

It must have been something in my expression that had Everette sprinting to my side. "Shelby. This is a good thing. You solved a case."

"I did solve it." I shook my head while trying to make sense of what was happening. "This was a test? The test to see if I could work with you? And I passed it?" Hope began to return.

"It wasn't a test." He made a pained face. "More like a game. I wanted to do something that would challenge you, get you excited, leave you feeling good about yourself."

"*A game?* What?" I shook off his attempt to hold my hand and pointed at the woman before me. "Hold on. Who are you?"

"Joanna. Bradford's wife."

"And you were asked to meet me here with your dog?"

"Technically, he's your dog. Everette got him for you. Tyr failed out of police training. A little too goofy for their taste, but smart and loving. In fact, if you ever don't want him, he could have a home with me. He's wonderful."

"So—so you were never in hiding from anyone."

"No," she said quietly.

I spun on Everette. "You lied to me."

He raised a hand in defense. "A white lie. The kind you

tell someone to make them feel better."

I swayed on my feet and shoved off his second attempt to touch me. "So, the man we met at the park? The one who said he'd met Joanna."

"I asked him to be there and tell you he'd seen Joanna. His name is Clay—"

"And the woman at the pet store? The one who suggested we come here?"

"Clay's wife, Lexi."

I blinked back tears of confusion as I went over everything that had happened that week. "And the man who came to the bed-and-breakfast? Was his name even Bradford? Is there a Bradford? Was everything you told me a lie?"

"That was Bradford. I really do work with him."

Joanna excused herself and stepped away.

I continued, "And he needed your help?"

"Not this time."

My hand went to my mouth in horror. "He was part of this game too, wasn't he? What the fuck is wrong with you? Why would you do this to me?"

Everette grabbed one of my arms. "You're not looking at this the right way. I didn't do this *to* you, I did it *for* you. Think about how happy you've been all week."

I ripped my arm free from him. "Don't touch me. Don't fucking touch me." I wrapped my arms around my waist and took deep breaths because I was about to hyperventilate. "The training? Have I actually been training for a job or was that a lie too?"

The pause before he answered should have been enough,

but he added, "I'm not in a position to hire anyone for the organization I work for, but the job wouldn't be what you'd need anyway. It's not safe. What you needed was the mental and physical boost that the training gave you. I didn't lie about that. Running, building up muscle, learning self-defense—all of that worked. You're happy again. That's why I came back. It's why I did all this."

I took a step back from him. "No. Happy isn't how I feel right now. I don't know what I feel. Everything I thought I knew about you . . . it's all a lie."

"No."

"Yes. Don't even try to gaslight me on this one. In fact, don't bother to say anything at all. I wouldn't believe you anyway. Just stay the hell away from me." I turned and strode away from him.

He stayed at my side. "Shelby, if you calm down and listen to me—"

"Calm down? This is me forcing myself to be calm when what I really want to do is . . ." I didn't know what I wanted to do to him, but I did want to get away from him. Far, far away. "Leave me alone, Everette."

Joanna approached with Tyr. "Is everything okay?"

"Get him the hell away from me," I snarled. "I am so done with him, and this place, and all of you." Tyr whined and pulled as if wanting to come to my side. I backed away from him as well. "All of you, just stay away from me."

"This is not how I pictured it going," Everette said urgently. "Shelby, you were so happy a few minutes ago. Think about that. That's what this is all about."

I shook my head and started walking off again and nearly lost my mind when Everette fell into step with me again. "Okay," he said, "you're angry. I get it. You don't want me to be the one to talk you through this. Call Megan."

"Don't tell me what to do."

"I want to respect that you want to be alone, but I also need to know that you'll be okay. Call Megan."

His concern for me only confused me more. My hands fisted at my sides and I let out a frustrated close-mouthed scream. "Don't pretend to be on my side when you clearly aren't. I'm so fucking stupid. I believed everything you said. Everything. None of it even sounded fucking realistic, but I wanted it to be true so much I swallowed all of it." Glaring at him, I growled. "I hate you. I don't hate many people, but *I hate you.*"

He blinked a few times as if my words had hurt him. "I'm sorry. I thought this would help you."

"That's probably a lie because everything you say is a lie." As nausea rose within me, I stopped and bent over. "Get away from me." In the ultimate act of humiliation, I began to throw up.

Everette took my phone from my back pocket, waved it in front of my face to unlock it. I attempted to grab it, but bent over again when another wave of nausea hit.

"Megan?" he said in a tight voice. "How quickly can you get here? I fucked up."

Chapter Twenty-Three

Everette

T HE NEXT FEW minutes were an absolute blur. Joanna handed Tyr's leash to me and told me to take a walk, or five, around the shelter. I didn't want to leave Shelby, but staying near her was clearly upsetting her more. I handed Joanna Shelby's phone and backed away.

Bradford appeared at my side. "Come on. Joanna will make sure she's safe."

I turned and fell into step with Bradford. "She said she hates me." The words gutted me as I said them.

"You'll survive," Bradford said in a harsh tone.

Part of me understood his lack of sympathy. I knew enough about his life to get that mine looked idyllic to him. I had two parents who loved me, had never lost someone I loved to senseless violence, and had a face that most people fawned over. Bradford had been alone before he met Joanna, he'd survived great loss and tragedy, and people tended to call the police when he showed up just because he looked dangerous. We were not the same.

But that didn't mean this didn't hurt.

I sighed. "I saw this going more like a surprise party. After the shock of it, she'd realize how amazing it is that people care so much about her."

"If it makes you feel better, although I never thought it was a good idea, I didn't see it going this badly either."

"She was throwing up. That's not your regular I'll-forgive-you-easily angry. I really hurt her."

Bradford nodded. "Sure looks that way."

It didn't seem possible. I stopped walking and turned to Bradford. "I don't hurt anyone. Ever. I've spent most of my life being so fucking nice I was miserable before I met you." Sensing my mood, Tyr whined and leaned against my leg. I gave his head a reassuring pat. "This isn't something I did without thinking it through. Even Tyr. He's perfect for her. She has anxiety at night when she's alone. Tyr knows how to search a house for someone. On command he can hold his ground against an intruder. But he's also calm and sweet. He's what she needs." When Bradford didn't say anything, I added, "How am I the bad guy?"

Neither of us had come up with an answer to that question before Clay and Lexi joined us. Lexi spoke first. "Joanna texted me what happened. Clay, stay here with Everette while I go see if there's anything I can do to help." Without waiting she left us.

Holding Boppy beneath one arm, Clay said, "Boppy, is that how you feel when I tell you to sit and stay?"

Bradford grunted. "Lexi has you well trained."

Clay shot him a look. "Tell yourself whatever you need to, Bradford, but you're right here with us."

The glare Bradford shot Clay was almost comical. Almost. Nothing could be funny when my whole world was crashing down. "Could the two of you postpone your pissing contest until we know if Shelby's okay?"

Clay's attention returned to me. "You know what always works? A trip to Paris on a private jet. Flowers. Jewelry. I can make all of that happen."

"You're not helping," Bradford cut in.

"Oh." Clay's stance mirrored his sarcasm. "And you are? What profound advice are you giving Everette?"

With a growl, Bradford folded his arms across his chest. "Shut up, Clay, or I will shut you up."

Clay didn't look intimidated. "Everette, what you're witnessing here is a man reducing to his most comfortable response to conflict—brute force. Joanna would never let him get away with that. It might be effective with criminals and strangers, but Bradford, you and I are friends. We know each other too well to do this dance. If you punch me, I'll buy everything you own out from under you and make you apologize before I sell it back to you. Now be nice because this isn't about us. It's about Everette. Are you here to help him or just to go round for round with me?"

"I'm here to help him," Bradford said between gritted teeth.

How was it possible that these two powerful and wealthy men were more messed up than I was? Clay wanted nothing more than Bradford to accept him and Bradford couldn't see that. I raised my free hand in a plea for a truce. "Although I appreciate both of you being here, this is something I should probably sort out on my own."

After a brief pause, Clay said, "When Joanna told us that you thought Shelby might need her friend, I sent a helicopter for her. She should be here shortly."

"You sent a helicopter for Megan?" Clay really did have too much money.

He shrugged. "It's the most efficient way to get around, especially with traffic. I've arranged for a space for them to land in the back field. They'll be taken back to the bed-and-breakfast where Shelby can pack up and leave if she wants to. I've asked the pilot to take them wherever they want to go."

"Why would you do that?" I asked urgently. "Shelby can't leave without talking things out with me."

Bradford put a hand on my shoulder. "Yes, she can. You'll figure out how to make it up to her, but if she wants to go, you have to let her go. Clay's right to respect that."

"Thank you," Clay said quietly.

Impatiently, I said, "I'm not saying I'd keep her here against her will, but shouldn't I have a chance to explain my side to her?"

They both shook their heads in unison.

Clay spoke first. "Lexi explained it to me this way: It doesn't matter how great of an idea we thought this was. It doesn't matter if we think she should have been happy that we did this for her. We're not her and we have to accept that people respond to situations based on the experiences they've had. Everette, you've had a good life. You expect good things from people because that's what you've lived. No matter how wonderful a family member seems to me, I would never send a child of mine off to live with one of them because I've seen the dark side of that. Bradford doesn't give a person a chance to come for him because he knows that when people do they can leave devastation in their wake. What we're seeing in Shelby is probably a combination of what happened to her parents with an added layer of what her life has been like since. A lot of people said things about her family that wasn't true. A lot of people let her down. I'm sure trust is hard for her. Taking all of that into consideration, it might be difficult for her to see that not all lies are a betrayal of trust."

I let his words sink in, really sink in and a wave of shame followed. "I wanted to be a hero—her hero. But I didn't think about how all of this might feel to her. And even when she was crying I was thinking she was wrong. But she's not."

Quietly, Bradford said, "No, she's not."

"How did I not see how much this would hurt her?"

Bradford looked from me to Clay. "We all forget that our view of the world is not the only valid one. You're not a bad guy, Everette, but I don't know if Shelby will forgive you for this."

Clay nodded. "When I don't know what to do, I throw money at a situation. For a long time, money was all I had. But I know if I had to choose between everything I have and Lexi, I'd choose her every time—every single time."

Bradford nodded. "I'd do the same for Joanna."

They both turned toward me and Clay asked, "Is Shelby that for you?"

Moments from the past few weeks flashed through my head. I thought of her crying on the bench by the lake. I remembered how good it felt to wake with her in my arms. Every moment with her came back to me vividly—working out, laughing, making love. She'd gone from being someone I wanted to help to being a part of me. "Yes. I love her."

Clay cleared his throat. "Hopefully that will be enough."

Even though I couldn't see Shelby, I looked in the direction of where she'd been. "I don't want to leave her while she's hurting."

"Part of loving someone is understanding when they need time to work things through," Bradford said, echoing what I was discovering.

Clay added, "She's not alone. You made sure of that. When she's had time to work this through, that will mean a lot to her—more than flowers or a trip to Paris ever could."

I nodded even though what I really wanted to do was go to her and beg her to forgive me. When Tyr made a sound at my side, I looked down at him. "Don't worry, Tyr, you're not alone either. I promised you a home and you'll have one with me unless she decides she wants you before she wants me."

Neither of the men beside me said everything would be fine and that Shelby would forgive me. Despite being as different as night and day, they both obviously had their doubts that she would.

Prior to Shelby, I hadn't known that loving someone could feel so good and so bad at the same time.

Chapter Twenty-Four

Shelby

AFTER FEELING ALIVE and refreshed, it was like someone was smothering me beneath a 200-pound weighted blanket. An invisible shield had descended between me and my emotions. I was aware that Joanna and Lexi were there and trying to say things to make me feel better, but what they said remained a buzz I felt no connection to.

Not since receiving the call about my parents had I felt so distant from my surroundings and adrift in my thoughts. The physical location of my body didn't matter. Nothing did. Would it ever again? Maybe feeling nothing was better than the hurt that kept side-swiping me whenever I thought things were going well.

I held the water someone handed me. I sat on the bench they suggested I rest on. They were probably concerned I might throw up again, but that danger had passed. Much like my brain, my body had shut off.

How long I sat there, I have no idea. It was long enough that both Lexi and Joanna stopped trying to talk to me. They stayed close, but ceased interacting with me.

"Hey," Megan said when she joined me on the bench.

I didn't look up from the grassy patch a few feet in front of me. I didn't want to be there, didn't want to need her strength yet again, and hated that my life was mirroring the frustrating childhood game of Chutes and Ladders. Just when I'd thought I might have been moving forward—whoosh, back to the beginning. Although it wasn't fair, I didn't have the energy to be angry about it.

"Look at me," Megan said.

I didn't respond.

She grabbed my arm and shook it. "Don't you dare hide from me, Shelby. Fucking look at me."

I raised my gaze to meet hers and tears filled my eyes.

Her hand tightened on my arm. "I don't claim to fully understand what went on here, but no one can fix you and no one can break you—except you. Don't allow this to break you. I need my best friend and yes, I know you hate that you need me, but suck it up. I'm here. And if I were hurting, you'd be right by my side. So, you can tell yourself whatever you want to, but I love you and you are stronger than whatever just happened to you."

I wiped a hand across the corner of one eye. "I hate him, Megan. I hate him so much it hurts."

"Of course you do. He hurt you."

"Yes, he did."

After a moment, she said, "You sounded so happy this morning. I just want to make sure I have the full picture of what happened. He didn't physically hurt you, did he?"

I looked away. "No."

"Did he threaten you?"

My gaze flew back to clash with hers. "Are you on my side or his?"

Her hand began to rub my tense back. "I'm team Shelby one hundred percent. You hate him, I hate him. But I just need to know what we hate him for."

I wasn't ready for that conversation so I stood up. "Can we leave? I need to get out of here."

"Sure," she said slowly. "I don't have my car. One of your friends sent a helicopter for me."

"My *friends*?"

"Clay Landon."

The man from the dog park. "He's not a friend. He just had a role in the game Everette decided I should play."

"Well, he must feel bad about being involved because the pilot said he's been assigned to fly us wherever we want to go for however long this takes to work out."

Shaking my head, I asked, "What?"

"Looks like we have a helicopter at our disposal for as long as we want it."

Tears filled my eyes again. "I have nowhere to go."

"Yeah." Her hand returned to my back. "I can see how you'd feel that way. What do you say we go back to the bed-and-breakfast? You can gather up your stuff . . . or stay there if you want. I brought some work with me and can do it remotely."

"I don't want to see Everette."

"I'll make sure you don't." Linking her arm with mine, she tugged me along across the grass.

The pilot of the helicopter met us and introduced himself. I greeted him absently, then stepped through the door he opened. I'd taken helicopter tours before, but this was a portable luxury office. Under any other circumstances I would have been wowed by the soundproof interior, cream leather seats, and wide windows.

Megan belted herself into the seat beside me. "Imagine owning something like this."

I shrugged.

She pushed my shoulder with hers. "Girl, you're upset, not dead. Look around, this is nice."

That brought a half-smile to my lips. "The owner is married."

"I know, but you've wandered into a wealthy circle of people."

As the helicopter took off, I said, "Everette still lives with his parents. The man who owns this is the brother of one of his friends."

"Can I meet that friend?"

"Also married."

"Damn."

I closed my eyes briefly, but a smile tugged at my lips. "Would you try to take this seriously? I'm falling apart here."

"I took it seriously enough that I left work and flew up here. What I won't do is blindly agree with everything you say. If you wanted that you should have called someone who doesn't know you as well as I do."

"I didn't call you."

"Ouch," she said without sounding offended. "You're

right, Everette did. Which is a point in his favor. He might have really screwed up, but he's not here telling you what you should or shouldn't think. He knew you needed someone and knew it couldn't yet be him. Are you sure we hate him?"

I looked out the window and answered honestly. "I'm not sure of anything right now."

"That's fair."

"For a long time I felt like I was drowning and then Everette came along and pulled me onto shore. I could breathe again. I didn't forget what happened, but it was beginning to feel like I could control how much it affected me. I felt— strong again."

"What happened today, Shelby? I have a basic understanding of what went down, but I need you to tell me."

Never taking my gaze from the window, I walked her through everything that had happened after we'd ended the call with her earlier. I described how excited I'd been when I'd spotted a woman with a black Labrador. I told her that Everette had wanted to come with me, but that I'd worried he might intimidate her so I went alone. I walked her through how confusing my initial conversation with Joanna had been.

"So, Everette did all of this to give you a dog? Did you ever tell him you wanted one?"

I temporarily hid my face in my hands. "I don't think so. I've never had a dog. I can't imagine that I ever said I wanted one."

"Okay, well, tell me what Everette said when you confronted him."

"He admitted everything. He admitted he'd lied about there being a job for me. He admitted that everything he'd said to me since he'd come back to the bed-and-breakfast was a lie."

"Hold on, why would he train you for a job that didn't exist? Was it just to get you into bed?"

I met her gaze and shrugged. "Maybe. I don't know. He said I needed the physical and mental boost of working out and learning self-defense."

Her nose wrinkled. "He wasn't wrong. You told me that everything you did with him made you feel good about yourself."

"He *lied* to me. Over and over and over again—about everything. It was all a lie."

"All of it?" When I shot an angry look at her, she raised her hands in mock defense. "I'm not defending him, just trying to figure out what his motivation was. He's gorgeous. If his goal was just to fuck you, it seems like showing up where you were might have been enough. He put a lot of effort into this."

Looking skyward, I searched through what he'd said for his reasoning. "He said he did it to make me happy."

"Holy moly." Megan chuckled, then stopped when I pinned her with a look. "I'm sorry. I just imagined if that were true and how disappointed he must have been when you lost your shit."

"That's funny?" Nothing about the situation felt remotely amusing.

"Did you hear his voice when he told me to come because he'd fucked up? He was shaken. I'm beginning to think Everette thought you'd love the dog, be grateful for the game, and the two of you would ride off into the sunset with you thanking him for saving you." She let out a pained laugh. "That poor man."

"I trusted him, Megan. I believed everything he said. We spent days looking for a woman who I thought was in trouble, but who was actually one of his friends. Poor him? *Him?*"

"You're right, he's a horrible person. And awful in bed."

Grudgingly, I admitted, "He's actually really good in bed."

"He probably doesn't even help find lost children."

Even though I hadn't been actively listening, I'd heard what Lexi and Joanna had been telling me about Everette when they'd tried to sell me on what a good man he was. "Unless his friends are all liars too, he did train with Bradford and does help find and return lost children."

"What an asshole, am I right?"

I frowned. "I didn't say he's all bad. I said he lied to me—a lot. More than I could ever forgive."

"You know what bugs me the most about him? I don't like that he came back for you like you needed him. You were perfectly fine on your own."

I rubbed a finger over my throbbing temple. "I was in a pretty bad place when he met me."

"And then he practically ignored you."

I shook my head. "I know what you're doing. Yes, he was

good to me. He was attentive and motivational and funny and sweet . . ."

"Bastard."

I laugh/cried for a breath, then said, "I thought I knew him. I thought I knew who I was becoming with him."

"And that was?"

"A badass. I didn't feel like a victim anymore. I felt like I could actually save someone."

"Shelby, you can."

And there it was, the fear I held the tightest to me. "I couldn't save my parents. I couldn't even save their public memory. I failed them—twice."

"You didn't fail anyone, Shelby. The only one responsible for what happened to your parents is the man who robbed them that night. And the people who write hateful things about you—they're just like him—not worth trying to figure out. There are good people in the world and there are people who are evil to the core. Most of us are somewhere in between. I am. You are. Everette is. Promise me something."

"Yes?"

"Don't make any big decisions based on how you feel right now. Give it a day. Give it a few days. Maybe you'll forgive him. Maybe you won't. But I've spoken to you straight through your time with Everette and I'm changing my stance on him. I will always be team Shelby, but I can't hate a man who's been as good to you as he has been."

Tears filled my eyes. "I'm so angry with him."

"I know, hon."

"I can't imagine ever wanting him to touch me again. I

feel like everything we did together was also a lie."

She nodded. "I can see how you'd feel that way—today. You may not feel that way tomorrow morning. All I'm suggesting is that you let yourself process this."

"I can do that."

"And then, if you decide you don't want him, give me his number."

I gasped and smacked her arm.

She laughed.

And I joined in even as tears streamed down my cheeks. "You're an asshole too."

"You know what they say—you are who you hang out with."

I chuckled, then sobered. "Megan, I needed you today. Thank you for coming."

"Hey, what are best friends for?"

She hugged my arm and laid her head on my shoulder. I breathed in our friendship and after the storm within me quieted, I said, "You can't have Everette, but after this I do owe you. We'll find you someone."

She smiled. "He doesn't have to be rich. I'd settle for a man who loves me enough to get all of his friends involved in some crazy scheme to cheer me up."

"When you put it that way, what Everette did doesn't sound that bad."

"You don't hate him, Shelby."

"No, I don't."

But could I ever trust him again?

That was what I didn't know.

Chapter Twenty-Five

Everette

THREE DAYS, SEVEN hours, and twenty-three minutes later my father wheeled himself out onto the porch of our home in Driverton. "There you are."

"Here I am," I answered without enthusiasm.

"Emmie and Nathan will be home this weekend. They have a break from school."

"It'll be good to see them," I said without looking up to meet my father's gaze. I loved my siblings, but didn't want to be around anyone. Usually, I was their biggest cheerleader, loving the stories they came home with and eager to celebrate all of their accomplishments. I didn't have the energy for that.

I didn't feel like doing much at all. Levi and Ollie had tried to drag me out with them several times, but the last thing I wanted to do was drink.

"I've been worried about you, Everette," my father said quietly.

"I'll be fine, Dad. I'm just reeling from a quick, hard crash back to reality. It stings, but I'll get over it."

"Ollie and Levi told me about Shelby. Sorry things didn't work out with her."

"It happens."

My father rolled his chair closer. "Here I am trying to get you to talk when I've never been good about expressing how I feel about most things."

"Dad, I'm fine."

He was quiet for a moment. "It's okay not to be. Life fucking sucks sometimes."

"Yep, it does."

"This isn't just about Shelby, is it?"

"It's mostly about her, but I screwed up, Dad. I let a few wins go to my head and started to feel invincible. I was wrong and I hurt her, but that kind of overconfidence could have cost a child their life." I stopped there, realizing he'd have no idea what I was referring to.

"You think you're the only one who's ever reached for something and failed? It's called adulting. It's humbling, scary as hell, and downright discouraging at times."

Not sure his pep talk was helping my mood. "That sums it up."

"But you pick yourself up and you go on. You know why?"

"No, why?"

"Because life is a gift—even if it comes with challenges. You're a gift. Every good decision you've made, every friend you've comforted, all the times you've chosen to care for the people you love instead of chasing something for yourself . . . all of that made the world a better place. If you think in terms of only yourself, life can be dark and lonely. But we're all connected. Am I making any sense? This all sounded better in my head before I started saying it."

I smiled. "It does—kind of."

"All I'm trying to say is that I'm proud of you. I always have been. I was worried about you when you were drinking too much with your friends. I was worried when I heard about what you were doing with Cooper and Bradford."

My eyebrows rose in surprise.

He continued, "Did you think I didn't know? Everyone in this town knows everything about everyone."

That was true enough. "Sorry I lied to you about where I was going. I've lied about a lot of things lately. I did it with the best of intentions, but that doesn't change what I did."

"You lied thinking you needed to protect us from what you were doing?"

"Yes."

"And you lied to Shelby because you thought she needed to experience something that you had?"

"Pretty much."

"This was a lesson you had to learn. Lies hurt, even when they're said with good intentions. Hopefully you and all of your friends remember that."

"How much did Levi and Ollie tell you?"

"More than I wanted to know. You know how they get after a few rounds of moonshine."

"You drank with them?"

He shrugged. "Like I said, I was worried about you." After a beat, he said, "But then I was real proud. My son is out there bringing children home to their parents. *My son.*" His eyes shone with emotion.

"Thanks, Dad. That means a lot to me."

"I can't say I understand how you didn't know that Shelby would be angry with the little game you played with her, but I know where your heart was."

"It was just my brain that checked out."

My father chuckled. "That can happen to a man when he falls in love."

My smile was pained. "I do love her, Dad."

"I know you do."

"When I'm with her, I feel like she and I could take on the world and win."

"Sounds about right."

"I pictured her in Driverton. I imagined buying a house near you guys, raising a family, giving her and our kids the good life you and Mom gave us."

He cleared his throat before speaking. "I'm not sure I live up to that high praise, but I always tried to give you all I had."

"You did. And that's why I've never minded helping out. Family and community—that's what matters. You taught me that. I guess I'm still figuring out how to do that for others."

"You're a good man, Everette, and that can be a rare thing. Shelby will be back."

"I hope you're right. I want to go to her and beg her to forgive me somehow, but I also want to give her the time she seems to need."

My father chuckled again. "Get used to that feeling, son.

That's pretty much marriage."

I laughed. "I'm telling Mom you said that."

"Please don't. I get in enough trouble on my own." He winked, then said, "Have you sent Shelby a text?"

"Not yet. I don't know what to say."

"Years with the woman I love more than life itself has taught me to keep things simple. Tell her you're sorry. Tell her you'll be there for her when she's ready to talk. Make coming home to you the easiest decision she's facing."

"That's actually not bad advice, Dad."

"Well, your mother hasn't left me yet." He gave his legs a pat. "And I put her through some tough times. What she never doubted, though, not one day of our marriage, was how important she is to me. That's the glue that kept us together. None of us will ever be perfect, Everette, but we don't need to be to be good people."

I took out my phone, gathered my thoughts, and sent Shelby a text.

Chapter Twenty-Six

Shelby

I'm sorry. I see now that any lie, even one told with good intentions, is wrong.

Whenever you're ready to talk—I'm here and missing you.

Everette had ended his text with his home address, email, and a contact list with numbers for the people I'd met through him, his parents, as well as the hometown friends he'd mentioned to me. I'd read the text over several times before showing to it Megan. "Why would he give me everyone's phone number?"

"Maybe that's his way of saying he has nothing left to hide?"

"I'm not going to call people to confirm his story."

"Yeah, I can see how that would get weird."

I'd spent the days, after leaving him at the shelter, rereading my gratitude journal and scanning through my memories of him, looking for something negative. Outside of not being honest with me about why he was there, everything he'd done had been good for me. When I compared my journal entries from before and after him it was clear that he'd been bombarding me with positive, empowering messages and they'd been working.

How much of that had been real?

Was there any way to know?

"I need to see where he lives," I announced. "What do you say we just go there?"

"We?" Megan asked in surprise, then smiled. "Okay."

"His things are still here. We could say we're simply returning them to him. It's a several hour drive. If we left early in the morning we could make it back the same day."

"Or . . ." Megan held up a finger to make a point. "Hear me out. We could go today and take the helicopter. The pilot gave us his number."

"We can't really do that, can we?"

"I think we can." Her smile was giddy. "I mean, we wouldn't want to offend Everette's friends by not taking it, right?"

Her smile was infectious. "You just want another ride in that helicopter."

"Damn straight. Just because this has all been traumatic for you and we may be deciding where you want to live, that doesn't mean we can't have fun while doing it. I'm going to ask the pilot if we can sample that champagne this time. I didn't dare touch anything on the ride here, but I think the drinks in there are for the passengers. I bet they have great snacks too."

I laughed and my nervousness fell away as I imagined her emptying the contents of the mini-fridge into her purse.

"You know you're crazy."

"Like I always say, we become who we hang out with. Don't even think you won't be munching on all those snacks with me."

I threw my arms around her and gave her the tightest hug. When I released her, I asked, "Are you sure you're okay with coming with me? How is your job handling you being away?"

"I sent in the project I brought with me and put in for a few vacation days. I won't be able to stay long in Driverton, but I can be there long enough to help you decide if you should."

A slow smile spread across my face as a thought occurred to me. "And to scope out Everette's friends."

Her innocent expression was the giveaway. "If we happen to meet some of his friends while we're there . . ."

I gave her hand a squeeze. "If this town is as great as Everette made it sound, you might want to move there, even if you don't meet a man. He said it's a place where children run free, people watch out for each other, and the sense of community is strong. You'd like a place like that."

"I *need* a place like that."

The raw emotion in her response had me hugging her again. Megan and I had always been each other's rock. I tended to be focused on goals, which had always worked to motivate her. She found the positive in even difficult situations. Both of us had struggled over the past year. I was only just beginning to see how much of her strong façade had been for my benefit. It was time for me to step up. "I'm going to call the pilot and ask him if we could have brunch served on our way up."

Megan's mouth rounded. "Brunch. That's ballsy."

I smiled and shrugged. "We may never fly in a luxury helicopter again. You're right, let's have some fun with it."

"Oh, oh. See if he can get us some of those little finger sandwiches. You know the ones that come on silver trays. I've always wanted to try those."

"You've got it. I need to call the pilot, shower, pack a bag, gather up Everette's stuff, and call the Allens to say we'll be gone for . . . we're not sure how long. Technically we could be home tonight."

Megan's eyebrows wiggled. "I can't see that happening, but okay."

Once alone in my room, I read over Everette's text again, and decided to let my arrival be my answer. When I called the pilot, he said he could be at a landing spot near us within an hour. Before ending the call, I thanked him profusely then gushed, "Have you ever had a friend stick by you when the rest of the world walked away? Megan has been that person for me. I don't know if I'm supposed to tip you or put in a good word for you with your boss, but if you help me make this a magical trip for her, I'll find some way to pay you back for it. Hell, I'll give you my entire Pokémon card collection if you have someone pack a tray of finger sandwiches for the flight."

The man chuckled. "I'm well compensated. How would you define 'magical'?"

"Outside of the finger sandwiches, I wouldn't even know

what to ask for. We're not fancy people and we're going to a place that sounds like a very small town."

"If you're comfortable with someone else being in the cabin with you, I can have it staffed."

"Staffed?"

"A discreet flight attendant can be provided."

I chewed the corner of my thumbnail as I weighed if I should voice my next thought. "Could it—would it be too much to ask for it to be a good-looking male? Maybe in one of those suits a limo driver would wear?"

"I'm sure I can procure one."

I added quickly, "Not to strip or anything. That would be too much. If you could just make it seem like having someone like that serving finger sandwiches and champagne is normal, that's what I'm shooting for."

"Anything else?" he sounded amused.

"No, I think that'll have her smiling. Thank you again. Really."

A little while later as I packed, I was filled with anticipation both at seeing Everette again and at what Megan's response would be to a hot man asking her if she'd like more champagne while she nibbled on finger food served on a silver platter.

And I froze.

"*I'm beginning to think Everette thought you'd love the dog, be grateful for the game, and the two of you would ride off into the sunset with you thanking him for saving you. That poor man.*"

Although it was nowhere near the scale of what Everette

had done by offering to train me for a job that didn't exist and then have his friends feed me clues to find someone who wasn't lost, I did wonder if Megan had been right about what he'd thought would happen. I couldn't imagine Megan not being thrilled by what I had planned for her.

Wasn't I doing what Everette had done?

And if anytime during the flight Megan realized I'd asked specifically for an attractive attendant and called me on it, I'd laugh and admit it. Neither of us would be upset because she knew I'd never do anything to hurt her. My goal was to make her happy.

Just like Everette had said he'd hoped to do for me.

Yes, he'd lied to me. The first time as part of his undercover alias, then because he thought it was what I needed.

What would it take to move forward and feel that his actions were as harmless as I felt arranging a gorgeous flight attendant for Megan was? I thought about what Mrs. Allen had said about happiness stemming from gratitude and took out my journal and a pen.

The list I came up with for what I was grateful for since coming to the bed-and-breakfast was much longer than any I'd written to date. Everything from Megan's involvement in finding it for me, to how I'd learned to protect myself from an attacker . . . Everette was woven in and out of so much of what I was grateful for—even Megan being with me and able to accompany me to Driverton.

I didn't want to go to Everette angry. He'd inspired me to get up and move forward even when it wasn't easy. When I'd felt like I had nothing left to give, he'd told me the only thing I wasn't allowed to do was quit. That's the energy I wanted to bring to seeing him again. Maybe we didn't need to rehash every way what he'd done had made me feel and I didn't have to justify my response. We'd both done things wrong and things right. Would I forgive Megan for making a mistake? Absolutely. Maybe it was time to apply that same level of forgiveness to not only Everette, but to myself. I wrote all of that in my journal, closed it, and tucked it into my luggage.

When Megan and I climbed into the helicopter a short time later, assisted inside by a beefy, well-dressed man, I winked at her and said, "You're welcome."

"*I see now that any lie, even one told with good intentions, is wrong.*"

It was a lesson Everette had learned, but I was beginning to see I needed to as well. I thought about all the times I'd told Megan I was okay when clearly I hadn't been. I'd done the same with Jeff and myself. No, I couldn't go back and do any of that better, but I could go forward as a more authentic version of myself.

Not perfect.

Sometimes not very brave.

But continuously striving for better—and maybe that was enough.

Chapter Twenty-Seven

Everette

"THIRTY MINUTES UNTIL she lands," I said as I paced in front of the bar at Little Willie's. "Was having them use your mom's field a bad choice?"

Ollie splayed his hands in the air. "If she and Megan decide to stay you know that's where there's empty rooms, unless you think she should stay with your parents."

That seemed like it would have been a lot to throw at Shelby. *Hi, welcome to Driverton. Meet my parents? I was thinking more like you should stay with them.*

"No. She doesn't even know I know she's coming. But she has to know, right? I mean, she's using Clay's helicopter to get here." I took a deep breath. "I'm going to meet her when she lands, unless you think I shouldn't."

"Dude," Ollie said, "you need to calm down."

Levi gave my arm a punch. "I agree. You bring that energy to her and she'll fly right back to Rhode Island."

I nodded then turned and gripped the edge of the bar. "Don't let me fuck this up." Giving them both a stern look, I said, "And stay sober while she's here."

"Oooooh," Levi said, "look at you, thinking we're not good enough to meet your girl."

"I never said that."

Ollie poured a beer for Levi. "No, he just thinks he's better than us now and he can tell us what to do."

Levi accepted the beer from Ollie and was lifting it to his lips when Katie whipped it out of his hand. "And he's right. Everette isn't better than you, but he sure does have his life more together. If the two of you plan to sabotage his chance with Shelby, and think there won't be consequences, you're wrong. Ollie, I will have your mother here so fast there'll be tire marks on your new menus. And Levi . . ."

He looked at her, eyes rounded.

"I'd never forgive you. You're better than this. Both of you. How about instead of being afraid you're going to lose Everette, you step up and help him make something of himself. I don't know about you, but I want more from life than this. Everette's making a difference. I want to as well. It's sad that neither of you feel the same." With that she slammed the beer on the bar and walked away.

Levi let out a slow breath. "Sorry, Everette. We were just playing with you."

Ollie poured the beer out. "I hate when Katie's right."

There was an awkward heaviness to the silence that followed. Eventually, I said, "You two are as much my brothers as Nathan is. And Driverton is where I want to be. I hope things work with Shelby and if they do I'd love to settle here and raise a family. I imagine both of you teaching my kids to fish, hunt, and sneak apples from Ms. Tissbury's orchard.

But I can't party like I used to and take everything as a joke. Like Katie said, I want more from my life than that. And I keep hoping you will as well."

Ollie folded his arms across his chest. "I don't have too much else that makes me feel good."

Levi's shoulders slumped. "Same."

I remembered being in that place and having that exact thought. It was a dark place with no easy way out. "I know Bradford can be a pill, but he gave me the kick in the ass I needed. He'd give you a second chance if you took it seriously." When neither of them said anything, I added, "Think about it."

I pushed away from the bar and was turning when Levi said, "Hey, you should meet her when she lands. And bring Tyr with you. I bet she feels differently about him this time. Ollie and I will pick up some donuts from Manju's and meet you there. It'll be our welcome to our town gift."

"I'll do that and thanks. I bet she'd love that."

Ollie raised his voice above the chatter in the restaurant. "Hey, everyone, we're heading out for a bit. Katie's in charge. Put your dishes in the kitchen sink so she won't have to. We'll be back in a few."

"Good luck, Everette," more than one patron called out. There really were no customers in Driverton, just family and friends helping to keep the only restaurant in the area open.

"Thanks," I said with a general wave. Ollie had been smart to pour that beer out. Otherwise, there was a good chance someone would have called his mother even if Katie hadn't.

There wasn't time to waste, so I headed back to my house to pick up Tyr. No one was home, but he happily jumped into my truck and sat beside me as I sped to Mrs. Williams's. On the way there I noticed a distinct lack of people but wondering where they were was a distraction I didn't have time for.

My stomach flipped when I turned onto Mrs. Williams's road and saw both sides of the street lined with cars. "No. No. No," I said as I parked in the first available spot which was a good distance down the road. Tyr barked in excitement. "No, boy, this isn't a good thing." I climbed out and Tyr followed, trained well enough to stay beside me so no leash was necessary.

Mrs. Williams waved to me from her porch. I waved back with a smile even though I felt like I'd just stepped in front of a runaway train. When I was close enough to speak without raising my voice, I asked, "What's everyone doing here?"

"Everyone wants to welcome the woman your daddy said you intend to marry."

Groaning, I ran a hand down my face. "With all due respect, Mrs. Williams, we're not at that stage yet. I'm still hoping she'll forgive me."

Leaving her porch to join me on the path beside it, she said, "Yeah, I heard about what you did. Your heart's always been bigger than your brain."

"Thanks?" What else could a man say to that?

She tugged at the short sleeves of my button-down shirt to straighten them. "You nervous?"

"Yes, ma'am."

"That's a good sign. A man should never take a woman's forgiveness for granted."

I looked down the path to where half the town was gathered on her lawn, some had even brought lawn chairs and blankets. There were kids in strollers, a herd of teens, nearly all my neighbors, my parents, my siblings and right there in the mix of all that chaos was Cooper with his freaking rich family. Clay waved when he noticed my arrival. I let out a pained laugh and waved back.

A deep voice at my side said, "This sure is a batshit crazy town, but I love it."

Bradford.

Mrs. Williams made a clucking sound. "Watch your language. Joanna, you warn that man of yours that God gave him the ability to swear, but he gave me the soap to wash that filth away as well."

Joanna laughed. "I'd apologize, Bradford."

"Sorry, Mrs. Williams. I meant no harm." That such a harsh man could soften and bend was a testament to the love we all knew Mrs. Williams's corrections were delivered with. She said it as she saw it, but only when she cared enough about a person to look.

I realized then how critical a person's perspective was. If I wasn't proud of where I was from, how could Shelby ever want to stay? Sure my neighbors acted like crazy relatives, but would I rather be in a town where no one knew my name? No. If someone came for anyone in Driverton, they came for all of us. That sense of community was why

Bradford had moved there. It was what kept bringing Clay back even though he had next to nothing in common with any of us. I glanced over the crowd again, squared my shoulders, and said, "I was hoping to introduce Shelby to everyone eventually, but I suppose this will do."

As I made my way toward where we'd arranged for the helicopter to land, I was stopped every two or so feet by someone wishing me luck or giving me tips on how to keep a relationship healthy. Levi and Ollie arrived with boxes and boxes of donuts. I was giving myself an inner pep talk when my siblings walked over.

Looking more like a grown woman than my little sister, Emmie rushed over to give me a hug. "Don't be mad," she said in a rush. "Clay hired Adarsh to cater this event. After Shelby arrives, we're putting out a dance floor and there'll be live music. This is the biggest thing to happen here since the frog race at Cooper and Amanda's wedding."

"It wasn't supposed to be," I said with resignation.

Nathan gave me a quick hug. "Dad and I were talking this morning. I'm graduating soon. With my marketing degree and your sculptures, we could double . . . maybe triple your income. Since that money came through from the government, Dad's going to be okay on his pension. You can finally get your own place."

Emmie added, "And I landed a full scholarship this year. You won't need to be making payments to my school anymore." She reached up and touched my cheek. "I think it's a sign that all of this is happening just when you've met someone. It's your turn to be happy, Everette. You've done so much for everyone else. We're all here to show you and Shelby that we love you."

I blinked back a wave of emotion. "Okay, I love both of you, but this is a lot." Looking around, I raised my voice. "Everyone, I need to say something."

The roar of voices lowered and I waited until I had the attention of most. "Listen, I'm so grateful that you're all here, but I'm not proposing to Shelby today or anything that exciting. She's just coming to see me and hopefully—"

The rest of what I would have said was drowned out by the sound of the helicopter arriving. Everyone began to whoop and cheer. Even Mrs. Tissbury stood and cheered. I turned to watch the large helicopter land.

I stood there wondering what the hell to do next when my father rolled up beside me with my mother. We exchanged a look and I'd never felt so seen. I wanted this to go well but it had taken on a life of its own and felt completely out of control. My mother pulled me down to her level so she could give my cheek a kiss and brush a piece of grass off my sleeve. "All the best things in life are a little terrifying. Falling in love. Getting married. Becoming a parent. Watching your child fall in love. It doesn't get easier, you just get stronger. And I don't know anyone stronger than you."

"Thanks, Mom." I hugged her then smiled down at my father. "I'm glad you're both here. This will either go well, or really, really badly. Go big or go home, right?"

"That's my boy," he said. "Plus, there's free food. No one was turning that down."

We shared a laugh. "So true. Well, if I can convince her

to get off the helicopter, I'll bring Shelby over to meet you."

The dust began to settle around the helicopter as the propellers slowed. Once they stopped, the door on it opened. Oddly enough a huge man in a dark suit stepped out first then held out his hand to guide Shelby and her friend down the few steps. That's what Clay had put at Shelby's disposal all week? I shot him a quick look. *We'll talk about that.*

Whatever irritation I'd felt fell away as soon as Shelby met my gaze. It didn't matter that the whole town was watching or that we probably had a lot to sort out before she forgave me. It felt so damn good to see her again.

Chapter Twenty-Eight

Shelby

A S WE'D APPROACHED a field where a large group of people had gathered, I'd asked the pilot to confirm that we were in the right spot. It wasn't that I was expecting our arrival to go unnoticed. It made sense that the pilot would have confirmed our plans with Clay and that he would have told Everette. Emotionally, I'd been prepared to be met by someone.

What is this?

"Oh my God, they've gathered to meet you," Megan said as she looked around. "You're redneck royalty."

"Shut up," I muttered in a low tone as I fought the urge to bolt back into the helicopter.

"Sorry, I probably would have handled this better if there hadn't been a second bottle of champagne." Her words were slightly slurred. "Or if I wasn't a lightwad—lightweight. I don't even know what a lightwad is. Do you?"

Flanked by two particularly good-looking men, Everette was striding toward us. Beneath my breath, I said, "You wanted to meet Everette's friends? Well it looks like this is your chance. On a scale of one to ten, how drunk are you?"

"I don't really know because you know I don't drink. This feels like . . . at what number does every man start to look really good? Because Everette's friends are hot."

I closed my eyes briefly. Nothing was going as I'd thought it would. When I opened them, Everette was in front of me.

The man on his right handed me a box. "Donuts?"

"Sure?" I accepted them. Not sure what to do with the box I handed it to Everette who passed them to the flight attendant behind us.

The expression in Everette's eyes when he turned back toward me removed any worries I might have had regarding if coming to him had been the right choice. He looked so happy to see me; I nearly threw myself into his arms. Only the knowledge that we had so many eyes on us held me back.

His friend said, "Obviously you guys have things to talk out. We just wanted to welcome you."

It was difficult to look away from Everette, but I did long enough to say, "Thank you."

The man on the other side of Everette said, "I'm Levi. That's Ollie. We're Everette's best friends and neither of us have any plans of drinking at this event. We're glad you're here."

Everette groaned, but smiled while his eyes seemed to plead for me to overlook the hundred or so people in the background. "I'm glad you're here too, Shelby."

Megan chose that moment to let out a long, loud belch that only someone who had downed several glasses of a carbonated liquid could. She ever so gracefully covered her mouth then burst out laughing. "Sorry."

Everette looked at Megan in concern and I regretted not realizing how much the champagne she'd had on the flight might hit her. We'd both been laughing with the flight attendant as he'd served her round after round between passing out the little sandwiches she'd requested. Unlike her, though, I'd chosen ginger ale because anticipation had had my stomach in knots.

I leaned in with a tone loud enough for only Everette to hear. "Megan doesn't usually drink, but she had a little too much on the way here. She's been my rock. Help me make sure she doesn't embarrass herself."

Nodding, Everette turned to all those behind him and said, "Everyone this is Shelby. Shelby this is everyone."

A large group of people said hello and I responded in kind. Forcing a smile, I returned many of their waves as well.

In a lower tone, Everette said, "Ollie. Levi. Code purple. Megan needs a little time to sober up before she meets anyone here."

Levi said, "I'll get her some coffee."

"I'll find her somewhere to sit down," Ollie said.

When our eyes met again, Everette said, "We've all been there. Some of us before church. We've learned to cover for each other."

When Ollie offered Megan his arm, she said, "You have the most beautiful eyes I've ever seen."

The flush that rose up his neck reminded me so much of Everette when we'd first met. Speaking softly, I said, "Hey,

Ollie?"

"Yes?"

"If you even think about trying anything with her, I will find you and make your testicles into a snack for her pet turtle."

Everette nodded in approval. "Beautiful and slightly terrifying. That's my girl."

My lashes fluttered at his words as I realized that was exactly what I was—his. "Thank you."

Everette added, "Megan is safe here. We take care of our own. And Ollie's mom raised him to be a gentleman."

Ollie side-eyed me. "That's true, but I also liked you a lot more before you threatened my boys. That's just not right."

Beside him, Megan gurgled, "She learned that line from me. Turtles and testicles. It just sounds like a good threat. Vivid. Sticks with a person."

He gave her a long look, then smiled. "You're a little spicy, aren't you?"

She poked a finger into the middle of his chest. "Like a jala-jala . . . peños. Siiiii-zzle." With a cocky tip of her head, she said, "I would rock your world."

Laughing, he said, "I'm sure you would. Let's go get you sobered up."

"Your tone is a little insulting"—she waved a hand at him—"and I would be offended if your eyes weren't so beautiful."

I bit back a smile. It had been a very long time, maybe since our first year of college, since I'd seen Megan tipsy.

Had the past week been as stressful for her as it had for me? If so, she deserved a good buzz.

Ollie guided her away to a nearby table where he pulled out a chair and sat beside her. Levi joined them with a Styrofoam cup of coffee for her. His friends were exactly as he'd described them. As I looked around at those who'd gathered, the scene also fit with what he'd told me about his town. Old sat with young, children ran free. This was a tight-knit community. "Did I arrive on a holiday or something?"

Everette stepped closer and put an arm around my waist. "They're here to meet you."

"Me?" Megan had joked about that, but I hadn't believed it. "Why?"

Everette cleared his throat. "I told my father I was serious about you. He might have told one of his friends, who told someone else . . . and now they all know. There are no secrets in Driverton."

"Not even your top-secret organization?"

"Apparently not even that."

I leaned into Everette, soaking in the strength of him. "I'm not angry anymore."

"I'm still sorry."

Looking up at him, I said, "I'm sorry too. I couldn't see the good behind the lies."

"I shouldn't have hidden it there." He pulled me closer. "Are you okay with everyone being here? I didn't know they would be and then they were all so excited I couldn't exactly tell them to leave."

I looked again in wonder, smiling at the number of people who waved each time I looked around. When my gaze settled on a group of people I recognized, I gasped. "That's Clay and his wife? Bradford and Joanna? What are they doing here?"

"Making sure you're okay. Lending me support because I was a wreck waiting to hear from you."

I glanced up at him again. "You?"

He bent and gave my cheek a kiss. "You have no idea." His expression tightened. "When you started throwing up and I knew it was because of something I'd done—I didn't know how to make things right. I didn't know if you could forgive me."

"I didn't at first either." Wrapping both arms around his waist, I hugged him tightly. "But I've learned a lot about myself recently. Not only does being angry not feel good, it slowly kills your ability to feel anything else. I don't want to rehash everything that happened. I want to move forward."

"Me too." He nuzzled my cheek and asked, "Does moving forward include being okay with meeting everyone here?"

I laughed even though I realized he hadn't been joking. "You know what? That sounds like exactly what I need."

Chapter Twenty-Nine

Everette

L ATER THAT NIGHT I drove a tired Shelby and a somewhat hungover Megan to Mrs. Williams's house. Mrs. Williams led Megan inside, but Shelby stayed on the porch with me and Tyr. When I held out my arms, Shelby walked into them without hesitation and laid her head on my chest. I kissed the top of her forehead.

"If you're not comfortable here, I can get you a hotel room nearby. Or you can stay at my parents' house . . ."

"Mrs. Williams is so nice. I'm sure we'll be fine here."

I chuckled. "If that's your impression of her, she definitely likes you."

"She did lecture Megan on the dangers of alcohol."

"That sounds like Mrs. Williams."

"And Megan lectured her on the fine art of getting to know someone before passing judgment."

I coughed out a laugh. "She didn't. How did I miss that?"

"You were getting Tyr water."

"Megan is still alive so I'm guessing Mrs. Williams didn't

hear her."

"No, she heard her. At first Mrs. Williams looked of-fended, but unlike me, Megan doesn't tend to get defensive. She genuinely likes most people. So when Mrs. Williams was puffing up, Megan kept smiling. It was weird to watch, but Megan is gifted at diffusing situations. And bringing out the best in people. I know she does that with me. I told that to Mrs. Williams. She seems to like Megan now . . ."

"There's nothing to not like. You choose your friends well."

"So do you."

I hugged her closer and murmured, "I hope so because I can't imagine my life without them in it. Driverton is a unique place. We're a community built on ideals rather than ethnicity or economics. When the lumber mill closed, a lot of families moved away. The ones who stayed and the ones who return aren't here because of a job opportunity or even because the town is the same. The opportunities here for work are near nonexistent and we change every time a new family moves in, but what doesn't change is the feeling of community. We've got people from all backgrounds and in all skin tones. Outsiders try to tell us we can't possibly get along as well as we do, but we don't care what the media wants us to think. We survive the long winters here by relying on each other. What Mother Nature brings together, no government or social media influencer can divide."

"That's beautiful."

"It is, but as you saw today, not much happens here that everyone doesn't know about."

She tilted her head back so she could meet my gaze. "I've experienced what it's like to live somewhere where your neighbors don't care what happens to you. It's not something I'm dying to return to. I received notice from my Realtor that my parents' home is under contract. Everything is set for the sale to go through without me having to be present. Soon I'll have money to invest in a new place."

I didn't want to push even though I wanted that place to be Driverton. "Then this is the perfect time to scope out what life would be like in a small town."

She hesitated. "Is that what I'm doing here?"

I kissed her. "I know what I want, but I also know my life is here. Before we make any promises to each other, you should take the time to see what that would be like."

She frowned. "You say that like you wouldn't care if I decided Driverton wasn't for me."

In the background, Tyr whined and I agreed with him. The conversation was taking an unexpected turn. "That's not how I feel."

She pulled out of my arms and folded her arms across her stomach. "How do you feel?"

"It's not obvious?"

She shook her head once. The expression in her gaze was guarded.

"I love you," I said.

Her frown deepened. "Don't just say it because you think that's what I want to hear."

"I wouldn't. I have no idea what you want to hear." Tyr whined again and I rethought my wording, but wasn't sure how to be honest and express my feelings better. She'd asked me how I felt and I'd told her.

She huffed and shook her head, tears filling her eyes.

I thought about my father's advice and about how no matter what, my mother never doubted how he felt for her. Saying I loved anyone was new to me. There was a chance I was doing it wrong. "Shelby?"

"Yes."

"I'm still figuring a lot of things out in my life, but I'm not confused when it comes to how I feel about you. From the very first time I saw you I knew nothing would ever be the same. I couldn't get you out of my head. I had to go back for you. One day of us together and my priorities shifted to you. I'm not good at talking about how I feel. I'll probably never write you a love letter or fly you off to Paris, but I found Tyr for you because I know you get nervous when you're in a house alone and he's trained to not only seek out what's hidden but also stand in defense of his owner. I'm opening my life to you, but not expecting you to choose it just because I want you to. I'm opinionated, stubborn, but loyal and hoping we can be best friends as well as lovers. If that's not the love you're looking for, I'll respect your choice, but that's what I'm offering you."

Her hands came up to cover her mouth and her eyes shown with tears. "I want all of that. All of it. But I'm so scared. I want to say I love you back. I don't feel ready for that."

Her words hit me like a sucker punch, but I reminded myself that her experience with love involved tragedy and loss. I could be disappointed that she wasn't where I was, or I could celebrate that she was in Driverton and giving us a chance. "Hey, guess what we don't have to do?"

"What?"

"Rush. I'm not going anywhere and I'd love to introduce you to what life in my small town is like."

Wiping tears from the corners of her eyes, she asked, "Why are you so good to me?"

"That's the love part," I murmured and opened my arms to her again. Without hesitation she stepped back into my embrace. Few worthwhile things came easily, and I was willing to put in whatever time and effort she needed to see that coming home to me would always be the easiest decision she'd have to make.

After a pause, she asked, "Do you think Mrs. Williams would let Tyr stay here with me?"

Emotion welled in me that nearly had me wiping at my eyes as well. "I know she would."

Chapter Thirty

Shelby

L IFE IN A small town took some getting used to, but not in a bad way. Megan stayed with me and Tyr at Mrs. Williams's place for the first few days, but her vacation days ran out and her time there ended. She left in Clay's helicopter, sadly without a gorgeous cabin attendant, which she said was probably for the best.

A few days later Everette and I had taken the helicopter as well, but only because it allowed us to drive my car back together. The short trip gave us time to see Mr. and Mrs. Allen in person to thank them. Neither of them had appeared surprised to hear that Everette and I were a couple. They even promised to visit.

The living arrangements weren't ideal, but we made do. Everette stayed at his parents' house. I stayed with Mrs. Williams. When we wanted to be alone Everette and I went for long, scenic drives. Okay, we drove to whatever local hotel had a vacancy and spent hours tangled up in each other. No one questioned us about those drives, though. Not even Mrs. Williams.

I couldn't see why people joked that Mrs. Williams was scary. Sure, she liked to remind people of the rules, but that was the role people expected her to play. When we were alone, sharing a morning pot of coffee, she was both kind and open.

We talked about my life before Driverton and hers before and after losing her husband. She told me how as a young interracial couple they'd worried they'd be judged and their children would never be accepted. While dating, they'd come across some pretty ignorant people—some even in their own families—and decided to move to a city where they'd be able to blend in better. They'd never meant to stop at Driverton, but their car had broken down. Too broke to get the car fixed and scared, they'd been welcomed by an older couple into the very home they'd eventually purchased. After they'd shared their story with the couple, neighbors had begun showing up with home-cooked meals and offers to help. Pete Glenford took time away from working at his father's hardware store to fix their car for free. It was then that she and Ollie's father decided to settle down in Driverton rather than continue on to the city.

"I'm ashamed to say I used to think horrible things about small towns," Mrs. Williams said. "I've learned, though, that they're only as good or as bad as the people in them. Driverton has a tough reputation in the local area. We don't put up with nonsense from outsiders. But there's a difference between being nice and being kind. The people in this town won't talk pretty to you. If your car breaks down going through here, they'll tell you all the things you should have done that could have prevented that from happening, but then they'll take you in, feed you a good meal, and get you back on your way if you have the manners to thank them for it. But you bring a bad attitude here—we'll tow your broken-ass car to the town line and leave it there."

She wasn't joking.

"The men around here are a proud lot," she said. "Everette too. It's their strength and their weakness. We raise good men, but sometimes they get confused and measure themselves by what the outside world values. After my husband bought Little Willie's, he fed a lot of people who couldn't afford to feed themselves. And that's why, when the restaurant struggles, people don't mind bringing their own food and still paying. Ollie doesn't understand how that's not charity. He's grateful for their generosity, but it makes him feel like he's failing me. We struggle with money, sure, but we made that choice every time we decided to help those around us. That's nothing to be ashamed of."

"No, it's not." My understanding of Driverton was clicking together. "Everette told me your husband used to feed Cooper too."

"He sure did. You should've seen how scrawny Cooper was when he first came here. Hell, a stray dog nearly starving probably looked better than that kid did back then. But he had a heart of gold and that's all we care about here."

Driverton was as beautiful when seen through Ollie's mother's eyes as it had been through Everette's. "How do you feel about Everette encouraging Ollie and Levi to train with Bradford?"

"Damn fools, all of them. Bradford has too much to live for to keep playing expendable soldier. Everette's too sweet to follow in his footsteps, but he doesn't see that yet. Do I hope it gets my son and his fool friend Levi to sober up and start taking their lives more seriously? Absolutely. But Ollie doesn't have the killer instinct like Bradford does. Now Cooper . . . he has it right. Cooper helps people and lets the law figure out how to handle the criminals. I worry that these boys don't have experience with how cruel the world can be and some of the people Cooper has brought into our lives recently think they're invincible. No one is." She turned and met my gaze. "How do you feel about Everette working with Bradford?"

I hadn't allowed myself to think too deeply into it. "When I thought I'd be joining their organization, it seemed like a good thing."

"Be glad you didn't. One day, if they're not careful, one of them is going to get themselves killed and I've never liked funerals."

Mrs. Williams's concerns stayed with me over the next week. It was in the back of my mind when I had dinner with Everette's family. It lingered and made it impossible for me to fully enjoy myself on the evenings we hung out at Little Willie's with his friends. Regardless of whether I won or lost at darts or pool, I kept wondering how these good people could possibly survive against the evil of the world.

How long would it take for someone, like the man who'd robbed my parents of their lives, to rob this town of its innocence?

That fear bubbled up and spilled over on my third week in the town. We'd decided to get something to eat at Little Willie's after returning from a drive. A bunch of us were sitting there, laughing over nothing, when Cooper came in with Katie's brother, Sheriff Tom. They asked to speak to Everette.

I'd wanted to hear the conversation and for the first time since I'd arrived in Driverton Everette said no to me. No. No discussion. No argument. I was still mulling over how that made me feel a short time later when he returned to the table and announced that he might have to go away for a few days.

That's when I said, "No." And his friends fled the table.

Everette sat across from me, taking my hands into his and said, "Shelby, I have to. This is what I do. You knew that when you met me."

I tightened my grip on his hands. "You're the one who said you'd opened your life to me. Do you think that I can't be trusted with whatever information they just gave you? Who would I tell?"

He looked from me to Cooper and the sheriff. "I know you can be trusted. I just don't want you to worry. Two hours from here, there's a town where people have started to go missing. No bodies have ever been found."

Fear set my heart racing. "You don't track serial killers."

"You're right, I don't. But the daughter of a friend was driving through that area and hasn't been heard from. Not for a long enough time span for the police to consider her a missing person, but we've been asked to find her."

I frowned. "Is this another game?"

He raised one of my hands to his lips. "I wish it were. No, this is real. I'm heading back to my house to get an overnight bag and heading out."

"I'm coming with you."

"You can't."

"Oh, I sure as hell can."

"No, Shelby. This could be dangerous. We don't know who is taking people, if they're working alone, or how they're doing it. No."

"If it's too dangerous for me to go, it's too dangerous for you to go."

A sadness I couldn't understand filled his eyes and he stood. "I love you, Shelby, but I'm going."

I stood as well. "If you leave, I may not be here when you get back." I didn't mean that, but I was desperate. I couldn't lose him, not when I was just learning to believe we could be something to each other. "Don't do this."

He leaned down, gave me a kiss that was warm and gentle and completely pissed me off. When he raised his head, he said, "I have to, Shelby. I can't go back to who I was—not even for you."

"What's that supposed to mean?" I asked to his back as he walked away. "Don't leave me, Everette. Please." I hated how much my last word had sounded like I was begging.

I sprinted after him, grabbing his arm, pulling him to a halt. It didn't matter that we had an audience. Fear overrode pride.

As he looked down at me, I realized I wasn't being fair to him. He'd pushed me to excel, to put my fears behind me, but he'd never pushed me to change or to give up something I cared about. I knew what this meant to him and how much he needed it. "Everette, I didn't mean what I said about not being here when you get back. I'm just scared that something will happen to you."

A little smile pulled at his lips. "Someday you might even admit you love me."

Gasping for breath, I said, "If you come back to me from this, I will. I'll tell you that every day. Just don't you dare get killed."

He pulled me to him and gave me another long, mind-erasing kiss, then murmured, "I will hold you to that promise."

Framing his face with my hands, I said, "Text me every hour on the hour. I need to know you're okay."

"I will."

"I'm serious. I can handle this as long as I know you're safe."

"Every hour on the hour."

"Yes."

"I promise."

There was a strength in his voice, a general confidence, that reassured me. I was in a much better mental place than I'd been before meeting him, but I still had panic attacks from time to time—especially at night since Everette and I were not yet in the same house. Tyr would come to me, though, when I was nervous and his presence would calm me.

I hope Ollie is okay with Tyr coming to the restaurant, because I'm going home to get him.

Chapter Thirty-One

Everette

WALKING AWAY FROM Shelby when she was begging me to stay was the hardest thing I'd ever done, but I'd meant what I said to her—I couldn't go back to who I was, not even for her. Who would I become if I sat there, playing darts and laughing with my friends while some woman was likely being murdered and I could have prevented it?

Even if we failed to get there in time, and Cooper had just reminded me there was a high likelihood with this one, I had to try. I'd picked up some things from my house and was on the road to the first place Cooper suggested I check out, when I asked myself if I should have let Shelby come.

My first reaction had been an unequivocal no. She was still afraid of unexpected knocks at the door. Tyr was the only reason she'd been able to move her baseball bat from the end of her bed to the trunk of her car. The last thing she needed was to be involved in tracking down what very well might be a serial killer—especially if we didn't find the woman alive.

I was only one town away when I sent a text to Shelby

reassuring her that I was fine. Her response was a photo of her sitting with my friends at Little Willie's with Tyr at her side. A man could forgive his friends for a lot of things when they were as good to his woman as my friends were to Shelby. I planned to thank them when I returned.

A few miles down the highway, my phone rang. Bradford. "What are you doing?"

"I'm assuming you know otherwise you wouldn't have called me."

"You're not ready for this."

"Locate. Retrieve. Return. This is what we do."

"I don't like this one. It's got the hair on the back of my neck up. I've read over the reports. There are no leads. Whoever is doing this, they're covering their tracks well. No bodies, no crime. None of the missing people have anything in common. Men. Women. This isn't one where you should go in alone."

"Bradford, I'm armed and you trained me well. If I find something, I'll call Cooper and you if you want. I'm not an idiot. I understand when to call for backup."

"Do you? I'm heading to your first location."

"I can do this."

"Everette, Cooper isn't alone. He has Tom with him. Don't argue with me. Just fucking meet me at the location Cooper gave you." Bradford ended the call without waiting for me to answer.

Whatever.

It wasn't like Cooper and Tom would have given me the best lead anyway. Funny how they wanted to protect me, like how I wanted to protect Shelby.

A bit more down the road, a sign caught my attention. *Little Johnny's.* It reminded me of Little Willie's. I wondered if it was the same kind of small place where everyone knew everyone. If so, someone there might have seen the woman we were looking for.

The parking lot was mostly empty. I sent off a quick text to Shelby before going inside, simply telling her that all was fine. None of the cars in the lot resembled the one the missing woman had been driving, but I decided to go inside anyway.

The interior of Little Johnny's was as unimpressive as the outside had been. It was a fourth of the size of Ollie's place and not well kept. A woman told me to sit anywhere. I chose a seat at the counter and looked over a menu. It was sticky the same way the counter was. I ordered a coffee and a burger, thinking both would be safe.

The woman looked me over from head to toe, but not in a flirtatious way. She gave me a feeling similar to seeing a long-legged spider on the roof of my car while I'm driving. The way something like that watches you. When you know you know. If she wasn't a killer, she could make a career of playing one on the big screen. Eeeesch.

She asked me if I was from around there or just driving through. I told her I was just passing through, on my way to meet a friend, but had seen the sign and decided to get something to eat since I still had a long way to go. Her laugh was more of a cackle and odd because I'd said nothing funny.

I didn't take even a sip from the coffee she brought me. I

used the time it took to make my burger, though, to scope out the other customers. There was one lone man who looked like he was sobering up from a party that had lasted into the morning. At another table, sat a young couple who looked like they should be in school rather than eating out in the middle of the day.

Normally, I would have asked everyone there about the woman we were seeking, but my instincts had me on high alert. I hadn't seen anything that warranted having Cooper or Bradford rush over. Still, there was something not right about the waitress and the place.

When she came out from the back with my burger, a man dressed in a filthy apron stood in the doorway of the kitchen and gave me a look akin to the one she'd given me. He was tall, lean, and as all-over sweaty as an armpit in the summer. I don't want to say that I'd convict someone just by their appearance, but these two had crazy eyes.

I paid for my burger in cash without eating any of it, making the excuse that I hadn't realized the time and needed to run. They both just stood there looking at me. I'm a big man, but I'll admit my skin crawled beneath their attention and I was glad to step back into the sunshine.

I should have gotten in my car and headed out to meet Bradford, but curiosity got the better of me. I decided there'd be no harm in taking a quick look behind the building. The bushes around a dumpster were overgrown, but beside it there was what looked like a seldomly used dirt driveway. I walked over to check out what was back there.

A hit on the back of the head sent me to my knees. A

second hit and everything went black.

When I woke I was cold and gagged with my ankles and wrists securely bound with duct tape. A short distance from me was the woman I'd been sent to find. She was tied and gagged as well and clearly terrified. I looked around. We were in the walk-in cooler. My guess was still at the restaurant if the supplies on the shelves were anything to go by.

I struggled to free my hands then my legs, but whoever had bound me had done an exceptional job. It didn't help that each time I moved my head the room spun a little. Shit.

The door of the cooler opened and the waitress walked in. Her crazy eyes lit up at the sight of me awake. She stepped closer. "You are going to be perfect. Just perfect. Both of you."

I tried to demand she release me, but my words were muffled by the gag.

Her expression twisted with some mockery of concern. "Don't be afraid, yes it'll hurt—a lot, but then you'll be famous. You just won't be here to appreciate it. I wish you could be, but what we do today will be entertainment for people all over the world—forever. And when Robbie and I are sitting in our big house, we'll play the video of you all the time, even when no one is paying us to. You'll be like our special friends because you're going to make us rich."

I shook my head violently and used all the strength in me to break the tape around my wrists, but couldn't. She made a tsk sound. "Save some of your energy for Robbie. He loves it when people don't die quickly." Then she returned to the door and covered her lips with a finger. "Now, quiet please.

We still have customers. But don't worry, we'll close early today."

The room dimmed again after her departure and I looked into the panicked eyes of the woman across from me. I wanted to tell her everything would be okay, but all of the thigns I'd had in my pockets for a situation like this had been removed. No gun. No phone. No knife. No lighter.

The only consolation I had was that I hadn't brought Shelby into this.

Chapter Thirty-Two

Shelby

SITTING AT A table in Little Willie's with Tyr at my side, I took a sip from my soda water and told myself there was no reason to panic. Everette had texted me twice since he'd left, but it was five minutes past when he should have sent his third.

Then ten minutes.

Then twenty.

I texted him but he didn't text me back.

When I'd first found out about Everette's *plan* to help me feel better, I'd felt betrayed and wondered if I could ever trust him again. Time with him and with those who knew him had reassured me that I could. Everette was loyal and reliable. When he made a promise, he kept it. When he'd said he loved me, he'd meant it.

I stood up and, with Tyr walking at my side, I went to the bar where Ollie was talking to Levi. "Everette's in trouble."

They both stood straighter. Ollie demanded, "What? Where is he? What did he say?"

"Nothing. He said nothing, that's how I know something happened. It's been twenty minutes since he should have checked in with me and he hasn't. Something's wrong."

Levi grimaced. "He's working with Cooper, Tom, and Bradford. I'm sure they have the situation covered."

Katie joined us. "What's up?"

My confidence wavered for a second. This feeling of dread was nothing new to me and it had shown its head when there'd been no dangers. Everette was out there on a real job. There was a chance he was in a conversation with someone that he felt couldn't be interrupted. How much did I trust my instincts? And how would I help Everette based on them? I chewed my bottom lip and absently petted Tyr's neck.

Love was a leap of faith I'd been afraid to take.

Trusting myself was the same kind of scary.

Everette might be fine and I would look ridiculous.

But what if I did nothing and he wasn't fine? What if he was in trouble and I let the risk of looking foolish or getting hurt stop me? My chin rose with determination and I looked each of his friends in the eyes, one after another. "Everette would never not text me. He knows how worried I am. He's in trouble. Cooper sent him to check out a specific spot. I don't have Cooper's number, but one of you needs to ask him if Everette is there."

Each of them took out their phones. Ollie called Everette. "He's not answering."

"I know," I said.

Levi called Cooper. "Hey, Everette isn't answering his

phone and he was supposed to check in with Shelby, but hasn't. Are you in contact with him? He's not answering. Okay, do that and call us back." After ending the call, Levi said, "Cooper is going to check in with Tom."

Katie chose a caller from her contacts. "I have Bradford's number. He'll know what's going on. He always does." She put him on speakerphone. "Bradford, it's Katie. We think something happened to Everette."

I pressed my lips together as grateful tears clouded my vision. She could have said that *I* thought Everette was in trouble, but she'd chosen to believe me without any proof that I was right.

Bradford's voice was gruff. "I'm where he was supposed to be. He's not here. And he's not answering his phone."

I gripped the side of the bar and sat down on a stool. "Something's wrong, Bradford. I feel it. What can we do?"

"Nothing," he growled. "We don't know who we're dealing with or how dangerous they are. I'll make a few calls. The best thing you can do is stay right where you are and let us handle this. There are already three of us in the area. We'll find him."

The call ended and collectively we fell into a silence. I was the first to break it. "I can't sit here and wait for them to find him. I'm going out after him."

"No," Ollie said firmly. "The last thing he'd want is for you to put yourself in danger."

Levi nodded. "He's right. Everette would never forgive himself if you were hurt because of a job he took. He'd never forgive us if we let you get hurt."

I looked at Katie. For once she seemed to agree with them. "I can't accept that," I said as emphatically as Everette had said the word to me earlier. "Everette needs us. I won't let my fear of anything be the reason I fail him."

Ollie's shoulders slumped. "We should have fucking trained with Bradford, Levi. Then we'd know what to do."

Levi turned to Katie. "Don't even think about it. It's too dangerous. If anyone goes after Everette, it'll be me and Ollie."

The look Katie shot me was pure determination. "I'm so tired of failing, so tired of thinking I'm not capable of more. I know you all feel the same." She looked down at Tyr. "Even you. What kind of dog fails out of police school?"

I stood up again. "Katie's right. I've been afraid to tell Everette how I feel about him. Most days I wake up afraid. I go to bed afraid. I haven't been a person I could be proud of in a long time. But I don't care about any of that. Every cell in my body is screaming that Everette is in danger and someone needs to help him. Why can't it be us?"

"We could retrace his route," Ollie said.

Levi added, "We know him better than anyone else. We know how he'd think."

"I have a bat in my trunk," I said and all eyes riveted to me. "Oh, we're going in prepared. What do you guys have that would help?"

On point, Katie said, "I have a bug-out bag. It has a little of everything from scissors to a medical kit."

"Good, bring that." There was no way to know what we'd need, although I prayed Everette wasn't hurt.

"I have a shotgun," Ollie added.

That sent a little shiver down my back. "How fast can you get it?"

He lifted it from behind the bar.

Levi added, "Mine's in my truck."

Organizing resources had always been a strength of mine. "Okay, let's take two cars. If we have to split up, we will. But for now, let's go where we know he was. On the way, we can call Cooper back and see if they have some way to track him or tell us what his last known location was before he turned his phone off."

Raising his voice, Ollie said to the people in the restaurant, "Everyone, listen up. Everette may be in trouble. We're heading out to find him. We'll check in if we have any news. Spread the word that we may need backup. If we don't find him quickly, have your cars gassed up because we will sweep this state, knocking on every door and stopping every car until we find him."

Both old and young rose to their feet, and I was overcome with love for the people of Driverton. Smiling through tears, I said loudly, "When we come back with Everette, he and I are going to get engaged, and we'll do it at a barbeque with all of you there."

Several people cheered. Some clapped. One little white-haired woman said, "In my day we waited until a man asked."

Katie grabbed me by the arm. "Stop, before you have me bawling. Let's go get your man."

I nodded and followed her out of the restaurant to my

car. We put Tyr in the backseat and followed Levi's truck out onto the road. Katie called her brother, Sheriff Tom, who tried to convince us to let them search for Everette first, then made her promise to keep him informed every step of the way. After that, her phone rang almost constantly with updates from Ollie as we drove. Bradford had someone attempting to track Everette's phone, but that would take time.

Katie was on the phone with him when Levi said, "Little Johnny's. That's kind of funny. It reminds me of your place, Ollie."

"Everette would have thought the same thing," I said urgently. "And maybe that it would be a good place to ask people if they'd seen the woman."

Ollie chimed in, "You're right. Let's check it out. Even if he stopped in and left, he might have said something about where he was going."

The restaurant was a tiny dive well hidden from the road. There was only one beat-up vehicle in front of it. We parked near the entrance.

"It's closed," Katie said, pointing to the sign.

In the backseat, Tyr circled around, barking. I scanned the area. "Let's check it out anyway."

Ollie said, "Katie. Shelby. Stay in the car. Levi and I will look around."

I opened the door to my car and called Tyr to my side. "Sorry. That's not going to happen." I went to the trunk of my car and pulled out the baseball bat and one of Everette's shirts.

Katie slung her bug-out bag over her shoulder and came to stand by me.

I held the shirt up to Tyr's nose. "Find Everette, Tyr. Is he here?"

Levi and Ollie, armed with their shotguns, joined us as Katie and I followed Tyr along the side of the parking lot to a dumpster in a cluster of overgrown brush. My stomach twisted. *God, don't let him be in there.*

Levi sprinted ahead and disappeared down a gravel driveway. He was back a heartbeat later. "Everette's truck is back there, but he's not in it."

Ollie took on the unenviable job of lifting the top of the dumpster and peering in. I let out a breath of relief when he shook his head and closed it.

Our attention turned to the restaurant's back door. Tyr kept sniffing at a spot near us and barked. I bent down to see what had caught his attention and a wave of nausea hit me. "It's blood."

Katie pointed to a spot beside it. "Those are drag marks. Someone was dragged to that door, and it wasn't a small person."

No. No. No.

Think. Don't panic.

I took hold of Tyr's collar. "We need to go in there."

Ollie tried the door. "It's locked." He peered through the small window. "The glass is so dirty I can't see if there's anyone inside." He pushed a shoulder against the door, then slammed his body against it, but it didn't budge.

"I've got this," Katie said and took out what looked like a

kit of picks.

"What are you doing?" Levi asked.

"I actually want to work with Bradford so I've been practicing lock picking. I figured it's a skill that might come in handy."

Damned if she didn't have the door unlocked in seconds.

"Holy shit," Levi said. "I had no idea you were serious about that."

"There's a lot of things you don't know about me," she said.

Ollie stepped forward. "Levi, I just texted Bradford where we are. He said we should wait out here, but I'm with Shelby—we can't. We have the weapons, so you and I will go first. When we're in there, Shelby, ask Tyr to find Everette. This could get ugly fast, but these people fucked up when they took someone from Driverton."

"They sure did," Katie said.

Even though I was scared, I didn't want to run and hide. I wasn't alone anymore. I wasn't a victim. I was part of a community, and together we could handle whatever we came across.

Ollie and Levi entered with their shotguns.

Katie and I gave each other one last look, then followed them inside. It was a dark, nasty kitchen with rat droppings that initially distracted Tyr. I held Everette's shirt to his nose again. "Find him, Tyr. Find him."

Tyr sniffed the ground then led us to the door of a walk-in cooler that was locked with a padlock. I didn't let myself imagine all the horrific possibilities of what we could find.

Instead I stepped aside so Katie could pick the lock.

Ollie and Levi stood guard as we opened the cooler door. Never had I seen anything as frightening or as glorious as a bound and gagged Everette, blood stained down one side of his head and onto his shoulder, but alive. Alive.

I rushed to him, removing the gag.

He barked, "Get out of here, Shelby. The restaurant owners are serial killers. It's not safe."

Katie took out a knife and cut the tape around his wrists then his legs. "No one is leaving without you and—" She looked over at the scared woman. "You too. You're safe now."

As she moved to ungag and cut the woman free, I helped Everette to his feet. "You're hurt," I said, inspecting the bloodied side of his head.

"It doesn't matter," he said in a rush. "Let's get out of here." His first step was unsteady. I wedged myself under his arm to help support him.

The woman stood and Katie guided her toward the door.

"Easy," I said quickly as Everette stumbled. "Levi and Ollie are here too. They're armed. And Bradford's on the way."

Everette shook his head. "These people are sick. They film the death of their victims. I think to make money from it. I don't know if they have guns. Get me to Ollie."

That didn't prove easy since neither were outside the door where we'd left them. When a shot was fired in another part of the restaurant, the woman who'd been with Everette started sobbing. I told Katie to get her outside and picked up my baseball bat.

A tall, thin man ran into the kitchen and froze when he spotted us. A surge of adrenaline must have pumped through Everette because he rose to his full height and stepped in front of me. The man grabbed a knife from the counter, waving it wildly in the air.

"Tyr, guard," Everette said. Beside me, Tyr took a protective stance.

"No," I said, but Everette was already closing the distance between him and the man. It was a fight that ended so quickly it couldn't really be described as one. Everette smacked the knife out of the man's hand and floored him with a power punch square in the face. When the man attempted to scramble to his feet, Everette punched him again, knocking him unconscious, then grabbed him by the scruff of the neck and hauled him behind him to the door of the dining room.

Baseball bat raised, I followed.

Levi burst back into the kitchen. "Oh, that's where he went, the little fucker. I thought he was behind the counter."

"I heard a shot," Everette barked. "Is Ollie okay?"

"Oh, yeah," Levi said with a smirk. "And we didn't shoot anyone. We just wanted to make it clear that we were serious. How many of these fruit loops are here? We've got some crazy-eyed woman out there. Is that all of them?"

"I think so." Everette swayed on his feet and handed Levi the man like he was nothing more than a lifeless stuffed animal.

"Shit, your head doesn't look so good. Don't worry,

we've got this." Levi dragged the limp man into the dining room.

I rushed to place myself beneath Everette's arm again. He steadied himself against me and said, "I need a minute. I'm still a little dizzy."

I hugged him tightly. "I love you, Everette. I love you so much."

He gave me a pained smile. "This is what it took for you to say it?"

I hugged him again.

"I love you too, Shelby." He kissed the side of my head. "Sorry, I didn't turn out to be quite the hero I thought I was."

"Don't ever say that again." I tipped my head back to meet his gaze. "There are more than one kind of hero and you are perfect just the way you are."

The kiss we exchanged was full of love, relief, wonder, and tears. When he raised his head, he vowed, "I'm going to marry you, Shelby Adams."

I smiled and gently touched the side of his bloodied face. "You can't propose here, I promised everyone back in Driverton they'd be invited to the event."

We gave ourselves the luxury of a moment together before wordlessly deciding we needed to join Ollie and Levi. The scene before us as we entered the dining room stopped us in our tracks. The ceiling had been shot out. The couple were duct taped together, back-to-back, until they looked like mummies with only their eyes and nostrils showing.

"Can't be too careful," Levi said. "And they had more

duct tape than anyone should own."

Ollie nodded toward the couple. "We were going to call the police, but Tom told us to wait until he gets here," Ollie added.

"You follow his orders but not mine?" Bradford growled from behind us. Everette and I swung around in time to see him approach, gun drawn.

"Bradford," I said with relief. "We found him."

"I can see that." He nodded, took in the scene, then holstered his gun. "And you did good. What happened here?"

Everette quickly rehashed what little he knew about the couple and what she'd said to him in the cooler. The more he spoke, the colder Bradford's expression grew until he looked as deadly as a coiled cobra.

He took out his phone and made a call. Without fanfare he said, "I need a clean-up crew at . . ." He gave the address of the restaurant. "And the interrogator. It'd be nice to get some names to provide closure to the families of their victims before we dispatch this file."

Katie and the woman the search had started for entered the dining room. Her eyes were wide and she was clearly in shock. Bradford ended his call and walked over to her.

"You're safe," he said in a deep tone. "Which is something that sadly can't be said for those they met before you. I understand if you want to call the police. If you do that, there'll be lawyers, a court case, and possibly a movie made about this filth. However, if you allow me the honor of handling this situation for you, I can guarantee you will never hear from or of them again. It's better if some problems . . . disappear."

She swallowed visibly, nodded, then whispered, "Who are you?"

"A friend of a friend of yours and someone who'd like to see this go away as much as you would. We'll get you home, get a doctor to look you over, and whatever else you need."

She looked around before asking, "How did you find me?"

"Everette did," I said proudly. "All we did was find *him*."

Tears filled her eyes again, she walked over to Everette and took one of his hands in hers. "You almost died with me. I don't know who sent you, but thank you for risking your life for mine."

"I'm glad we're both still here." He gave her hand a squeeze before releasing it, then looked around. "We wouldn't be without my friends. Thank you."

Ollie nodded toward me. "It's Shelby you should really thank. We'd probably still be at Little Willie's if she hadn't sensed you were in trouble."

When his attention returned to me, so much love was in his eyes I nearly burst into tears. "You saved me."

Smiling up at him, I said, "You saved me first."

Chapter Thirty-Three

Everette

T HE NEXT FEW hours were a blur of having a few stitches put in my scalp, returning to Driverton, then reassuring everyone that, although I had a concussion, I'd live. When the flurry of visits finally ended, my parents gave me a good talk on how careful I should be in the future, both gave Shelby long emotional hugs, then retired inside taking Tyr with them.

Nathan and Emmie made a fire in the backyard before heading inside as well. Levi, Ollie, Katie, Shelby, and I settled around the firepit. I sat on the large wooden swing. Shelby curled up on my lap. It didn't feel like the worst day of my life.

"Anyone else wondering what's going to happen to the couple we handed over to Bradford?" Levi asked.

I shook my head. "Not really, but I discovered a few things about myself today."

Shelby adjusted herself so she could see my face. "And what were those?"

Looking down into her beautiful eyes, I said, "I have a

lot to live for. And a lot to learn." She cupped one side of my face. "And that my narrow concept of what is and isn't heroic needs some modifying. When I left you at Little Willie's, Shelby, I was selfishly chasing who I thought I needed to be."

She gave me a gentle kiss. "There was nothing selfish about wanting to save that woman. I understood why you needed to go." She took a deep breath. "And I understood why you thought I shouldn't go with you. I wasn't ready."

I rested my forehead on hers. "No one was ready for today."

"I was," Katie said. "Did you all not see me open those locks like I was born to?"

"That was impressive," Ollie said.

"And not a skill I'd expect from the little sister of the sheriff," Levi joked.

Ollie leaned forward with his elbows on his knees. "Speaking of skills, I'm going to ask Bradford to give me a second chance. I'd like to train with him."

"Me too," Levi added.

Katie smiled. "Me three."

"Before you do," I said. "We won today, but easily could have lost. Some of the people Bradford deals with would make that couple look like amateurs. I want to have a family and be around to raise them. Today shook me. It's not just that I don't want to die, but I also don't want the blood of others on my hands."

For a moment no one said anything. Shelby turned my face so I was looking down at her again. "Remember what I said about there being different kinds of heroes? You can still do good without putting yourself in danger. You're gifted at finding people. You're kind. People feel safe around you. And you have really good instincts when it comes to knowing how to help people. So, maybe you don't want to do the retrieval part. Maybe locate and return."

Katie said, "Cooper draws the line at hurting anyone and now that he has Amanda and the baby, he's more careful. I agree with Shelby. Trying to be Bradford would probably get us all killed. Wouldn't it be better if we played to the strengths we have? I don't want to be in a shootout, either, but I'd like to learn how to defend myself, and I think I'd be good at following up with people we've helped to make sure they're okay."

"I felt good about what we did today and good about myself. I'm ready to put down the beer and see what I'm capable of," Levi said quietly.

"So am I." Ollie nodded.

"Then Bradford is where you should start. Training with him was the boost I needed." I hugged Shelby to me. "It's been a journey for me, but I wouldn't change a thing about it."

Shelby snuggled closer. "I'm good at data analysis and resource distribution. If those skills can help out in any way, count me in."

"Count you in for what?" Clay asked as he approached with Boppy under one arm and Lexi at his side.

"Clay," I exclaimed then waved a hand toward my head and Shelby. "I'd get up but . . ."

"No worries," he said. "Hope you don't mind that we came by unannounced. I just heard how your day went and wanted to make sure you were okay."

"I've been better." I smiled at Shelby. "But I've been much, much worse. This is a casual celebration of the fact that none of us died today. You're welcome to join us."

Ollie grabbed chairs for both Clay and his wife. "Sit down and let us tell you the tale of how we saved a woman's life. All of us."

Each time Ollie told the story it was more graphic, dangerous, and heroic—and yet, somehow perfect. When he stopped to take a breath, Clay asked, "So, is this something you see yourself doing again?"

I made a pained face. "Not exactly this, but we're all on the same page that we'd like to keep doing what we can to help people."

Lexi touched Clay's arm. "You should ask them if you can join them." Her loving expression reminded me of when he'd told me she was the only one who made him feel valued.

Shelby exchanged a look with me, and it was as if we could read each other's minds. She said, "We were just talking about how it's always better when we do things together and if we each bring our strengths to the table, we'd be capable of amazing things."

I added, "Clay, we're starting this from the ground up. If you'd like to be part of it, we'd love to have you."

His face lit up. "If you're serious, I already have a slew of ideas. The deserted police station would be the perfect headquarters. We could tunnel out a section of the city beneath it, fill it with cutting-edge technology, and leave the original building as a front."

Lexi clapped her hands together. "Like Batman's secret cave. Can you imagine how fun that would be to design?"

Clay continued, "Forget about rental cars and burner phones. Think encrypted everything and untraceable technology all run by an off-grid AI."

Although I loved the idea, I felt something needed to be said. "Clay, we're not asking you to join us because you have money. We like you."

After an emotional moment, Clay cleared his throat. "We'll talk. For now, is it true that Shelby is still staying with Mrs. Williams?"

It was something I wasn't particularly proud of. "For now. I'm saving up for a house."

Shelby added, "I can help with that." She blushed. "I mean, we're practically engaged—just waiting on the ask."

"Yes, we are," I assured her with a kiss and a smile. "And I'd already have popped the question, if you hadn't told everyone they could see me do it."

Shelby laughed and explained to Clay what she'd said at Little Willie's before setting off to find me. "I was excited."

Lexi cooed, "An engagement party. We love planning those. Shelby, can we host one for you?"

"Umm—" Shelby looked from Lexi to me. "That seems like too much."

Clay put his arm around his wife. "They have plenty of money to host the party on their own. Remember? I bought that wooden carving from Everette's mom."

Lexi smiled. "Oh, yes, the one Bradford helped make."

"Which one?" I asked, wondering if the bump on my head had caused me to forget something.

Clay smirked. "Just a little something your mother found in the back of a shed. She said Bradford had helped you finish it a few months ago. I took one look at it and knew I had to have it. Your mother is quite the salesperson. I don't know that I've ever paid so much for a statue of a bear, but I'm having a little plaque made for it with Bradford's name on it and that will make it priceless."

"You can't do that, Clay; I hid it for a reason. Bradford's been good to me and I didn't want to hurt his feelings. He was trying to help. I'll pay you back every cent you gave my mother."

Shelby touched my cheek. "Everette, you have a beautiful soul."

Clay pursed his lips.

Lexi laughed. "Clay, tell him you'll give it back."

Looking a little like a sullen child, Clay said, "Only if Everette lets me install a secret underground base beneath the police station." He huffed. "And maybe build him a house."

"Clay." I laughed. He couldn't be serious. "Sounds like a fair trade. Drop off the statue and you can build me a secret lair and a house."

"And throw you an engagement party," Clay added as he glanced down at his manicured nails. "Lexi loves planning parties and making her happy makes me happy."

"Sure," I joked. "Whatever. I'll write you a check for the

statue and you're welcome to do whatever makes you and Lexi happy."

"Really?" Clay asked, eyebrows raising. "Ollie, I have an idea for Little Willie's."

"No," Ollie said.

"Rude," Clay said to Boppy who seemed to agree.

Shelby perked up and asked, "Hey, Clay. Do you have any single friends I could introduce Megan to?"

I coughed back a laugh at Ollie's expression. He hadn't said anything about Megan, but he sure didn't look like he liked the idea of her being introduced to some rich guy.

Clay's hand came to his chest and he beamed with pride. "There is no better matchmaker than I."

"I'm single as well," Katie said, waving her hand.

Levi stood so fast his chair toppled over behind him and it was all I could do to not laugh. My friends were nuts, batshit crazy. Ollie glared at him. I dipped my head and whispered in Shelby's ear, "Life in a small town—you sure you can handle it?"

She turned her head to whisper back, "With you by my side I can handle anything."

And I fell in love with her all over again.

Epilogue

Shelby

A WEEK LATER, I looked down at the modest ring on my finger and then back up at Everette. "Are we supposed to kiss now? With everyone watching?"

"They'd be disappointed if we didn't."

I pulled his face down to mine, went up onto my tiptoes and kissed my new fiancé in front of the crowd gathered on Mrs. Williams's lawn. She'd insisted on the location and there probably weren't two more stubborn people in town than Clay and her. Together she and Lexi had compromised between lawn chairs and more opulent furnishings. The result was stunning without being off-putting to the people in town who might never be able to afford anything as grand. The food was a combination of catered and potluck.

When the kiss ended, several people cheered. Slowly everyone's attention slid from us to each other. Within the warmth of Everette's embrace, I said, "I can't believe Clay and Lexi did this for us."

"I can't believe he flew in a prince for Megan or that she doesn't look all that impressed by him," Everette murmured.

I glanced over to where she was standing with the attractive royal. Her forced smile told me she was bored but being polite. "Megan jokes about wanting to meet someone with money, but she's too level-headed for that. We both had parents who chose their partners well. Hers are still happily married. She won't settle for less than that."

"I know the feeling. I wanted everything—the lover, the friend, the partner in crime."

My gaze flew back to meet his and I smiled. "I wanted all the same . . . along with a top-secret job. Clay told me I'm the ideal person to help him take his sketches for headquarters from concept to reality. I do love making task lists and organizing projects. It'll be a challenge I'll enjoy."

Everette's eyebrows rose. "I thought he was joking, but he also bought what he says will be our wedding present: a plot of land next to Cooper's. Until it's built, he brought in one of those double-decker luxury trailers and said we could stay there. Mrs. Williams may call you a hussy, but what do you think?"

"Mrs. Williams and I are tight. And she's probably ready to have her house back to herself."

Looking out over the lawn where the Allens were sitting with his parents, Everette said, "If you move out today, I bet the Allens would use that room to stay a couple of days. They seem to be fitting right in here."

My gaze wandered from there to where Bradford was holding court with Ollie, Levi, and Katie. Since his expression never gave away much of what he was thinking, he was either excited they'd all decided to train with him or suffering in a slow, small-town hell. Either way, his wife smiled on from her place beside him and I knew she had to be glad he'd found Driverton. Someone like Bradford needed to be around wholesome, loyal people—people who were still shocked by the underbelly of humanity. Word on the street was, she and Bradford were trying to have a baby and I couldn't imagine a better place for them to raise a family.

Just as I couldn't for my own family.

There would never be a day when I didn't miss my parents, but I had to believe they were smiling down and proud of how far I'd come. They would have loved these people—especially Everette. They wouldn't have understood how starting each day together with a run could be as peaceful as when they'd sat side by side reading books, but for Everette and me it was.

Nothing about Driverton was what I once would have thought I wanted, yet I couldn't imagine living anywhere else. In some ways the town was changing, but according to Mrs. Williams, that was the norm. Nothing ever stayed the same, but when it came to Driverton, everything that was important—their core values, their sense of community, their ability to welcome people in regardless of their differences—that remained constant.

From several yards away, Clay caught my eye and smiled. He said he wanted to plan our wedding, and so far, I'd politely declined the offer.

I was wavering, though, because it's not every day a woman is offered her own fairy godfather extraordinaire and Lexi promised she'd keep him somewhat in check. My only request would be that Tyr be included and wear a bow tie.

I mouthed, "Yes" to Clay. He smiled and raised a glass to me, then said something to Lexi and she did the same.

Everette bent and asked me, "What's that about?"

I laughed, hugged him, and said, "You did say I could plan the wedding however I wanted to, right?"

He looked from me to Clay and said, "Oh, boy."

The End

Don't want the story to end? Read on with Levi: Driverton 2

Driverton's bad boy has no desire to be a hero, but there's one woman who just might be able to change his mind.

Don't miss a release, a sale or a bonus scene. Sign up for my newsletter today.

forms.aweber.com/form/58/1378607658.htm

More books By Ruth Cardello

The Legacy Collection:

The Andrades:

The Barrington Billionaires:

The Westerlys Series:

Corisi Billionaires:

The Lost Corisis:

The Switch Series:

Twin Find Series:

Bachelor Tower Series:

Lone Star Burn Series:

Temptation Series:

About the Author

Ruth Cardello was born the youngest of 11 children in a small city in southern Massachusetts. She spent her young adult years moving as far away as she could from her large extended family. She lived in Boston, Paris, Orlando, New York—then came full circle and moved back to New England. She now happily lives one town over from the one she was born in. For her, family trumped the warmer weather and international scene.

She was an educator for 20 years, the last 11 as a kindergarten teacher. When her school district began cutting jobs, Ruth turned a serious eye toward her second love—writing and has never been happier. When she's not writing, you can find her chasing her children around her small farm, riding her horses, or connecting with her readers online.

Contact Ruth:

Website: RuthCardello.com
Email: RCardello@RuthCardello.com
FaceBook: Author Ruth Cardello
Twitter: @RuthieCardello

Made in United States
Orlando, FL
18 December 2023

41268046R00166